UNDER THE KNIFE

A vicious serial killer haunts the bayous of Louisiana. The only person who can catch him is FBI Agent Kate Palmer. But Kate's specialised work has taken its toll on her and she's facing burnout. Worse still, she's about to rekindle a relationship with the only man she ever loved when the Bayou Butcher strikes again — terrifyingly close to home. For Kate, that makes it personal — it might also be just the thing it takes to break her completely

STEVE HAYES
& DAVID WHITEHEAD

◆

UNDER THE KNIFE

Complete and Unabridged

LINFORD
Leicester

First published in Great Britain

First Linford Edition
published 2012

British Library CIP Data

Hayes, Steve.
  Under the knife.- -(Linford mystery library)
  1. Serial murder investigation- -Louisiana- -
  Fiction. 2. Suspense fiction.
  3. Large type books.
  I. Title II. Series III. Whitehead, David, 1958 –
  823.9'2–dc23

  ISBN 978–1–4448–0969–5

Published by
F. A. Thorpe (Publishing)
Anstey, Leicestershire

Set by Words & Graphics Ltd.
Anstey, Leicestershire
Printed and bound in Great Britain by
T. J. International Ltd., Padstow, Cornwall

This book is printed on acid-free paper .

For Robbin and Janet

1

The alligator measured twelve feet from snout to tail and weighed almost seven hundred pounds. It lay half-submerged in the reeds beside a narrow trail that ran alongside the river, only its eyes and nostrils visible above the surface. As befitted a creature with such a slow metabolic rate it lay perfectly still, content simply to wait for its next unsuspecting meal to pass within reach.

That next meal, unless fate decreed otherwise, would be a little girl in a wrinkled brown tank dress and pale pink water shoes, whose name was Marie Gaspard.

Of course, death was no stranger to these bayous of eastern Louisiana. Unlike other swamps, time had hardly touched this near-pristine wilderness known as Honey Island. Its profusion of cypress, tupelo-gum, red maple and buttonbush thrived unchecked — as did the abundant wildlife. Bald eagles, pelicans, snapping turtles, water moccasins and rare red wolves ... they all roamed free in this untamed Eden, while its sluggish green waters teemed with fish ... and alligators.

Marie Gaspard was a pretty Cajun child of eight, small for her age, with long tawny hair framing an oval, sunburned face that looked older than her years. As she followed the misty trail ever closer to the waiting predator, she scolded the rag doll in her arms with comical severity.

'*Vous êtes une mauvaise fille*, Chloe. An' I got a half mind to spank you.'

The 'gator watched her approach through flat, unblinking eyes.

'Don'tcha know you can get *lost* out here?' the girl continued, echoing the warning her mother had repeatedly given her in the past. 'Be days 'fore I found you, an' by then you be supper for *le cocodrie*.'

She walked on, getting closer all the time to the submerged alligator.

The hungry reptile prepared to explode out of the water and clamp its jaws around the girl's legs.

Twelve feet, ten, nine — only eight feet separated Marie from her fate when, unexpectedly, a baby-faced man in his early twenties dropped out of the trees and landed in her path.

'Boo!'

He was a big slouch, easily six feet, dressed in a white cottonade shirt, old patched bib-and-brace overalls and thick-soled lace-up boots. He had a long nose and a wide, thick-lipped mouth above a pointed chin. Below his thick, sandy brows, his eyes were different colors — the left one blue, the right one gray-blue. He wore a ragged baseball cap pulled low over his long straggly sandy-blond hair.

Startled, Marie stopped and clutched the doll protectively to her chest. Her big brown eyes widened with fear until she recognized the man: Nash Guidry, one of the two mirror twins who lived along Middle Creek.

Scowling, she turned her doll toward him and said disapprovingly: 'Chloe say it ain't polite to scare folks, Nash.'

'I ain't Nash,' said the man, avoiding her gaze shyly. 'I be Noah. Look.'

He took off his old baseball cap to show that his sandy-blond hair was parted on the right side, and began to dance a weird, floppy-armed kind of *fais do do.*

Marie clapped her hands, delighted by his antics. 'You are *motie foux!*' she laughed. '*Motie foux!*'

'*Oui, oui!*' said the man pretending to be Noah Guidry, the string of 'gator teeth around his neck clicking as he danced. 'I *am* half crazy!'

Scooping her up, he swung her around. '*Whoeee!*' he cried. 'See Noah dance . . . hear Noah laugh . . . ha, ha, ha! Give Noah a big kiss.'

He kissed her forehead, swung around once more and set her down gently. Then, putting his cap back on, he continued his stumbling, idiotic dance.

But Marie wasn't fooled. 'Why for you pretend to be Noah?' she asked.

''Cause I *am* Noah,' he said in Noah's familiar sing-song whine.

Marie giggled, held her doll to her ear

4

as if it was whispering to her. She then turned back to him. 'Chloe say if you be Noah, why not you have Noah's eyes? They be opposite to yours.' Before he could reply, she added: ''Sides, you not wearin' Noah's cap. Noah's cap says *John Deere* on it.'

Deflated, Nash Guidry straightened out of his brother's slouching, cowering posture, squared his shoulders and lost his dim-witted expression. Then, theatrically doffing his cap, he bowed to the doll.

'Shame on you, Miss Chloe. You spoiled my little charade.'

'She mean no harm,' said Marie. 'Do not be *colere* with her, *s'il vous plait*.'

He smiled disarmingly, showing his big yellow teeth. 'I'm not angry.'

'Promise?'

'Promise an' eat 'gator eggs if I lie.'

Marie giggled, won over by his charm. 'Chloe like you much better when you be Nash. Say your hair looks silly combed on the wrong side.'

'I'll remember that,' Nash said. 'I want Chloe to like me. Now,' he bent down

5

and opened his arms to her, 'c'mon, *cher* Marie. Be my best girl and I'll take you home. Give you a big surprise.'

Her eyes became saucers. 'Surprise? What surprise?'

'That's for me to know,' he teased, 'an' you to find out. Now, you coming with me or not?'

'*Oui, oui,* I come.'

Nash swung her up onto his shoulders and carried her farther along the water's edge to where he'd left his small, homemade pirogue.

★ ★ ★

The Gaspard cabin was little more than a pile of cypress boards, bleached white by the sun, built on a spit of dry land that every rainy season was in danger of flooding. It was a boxy, single-story structure with small, dark windows and plank walls crowned by a sagging, badly-repaired roof of pine shakes.

The nearby shed was a miniature copy of the cabin, except that it was surrounded by racks draped with the pelts of dead animals. A small mound of skinned and gutted carcasses lay nearby, their guts dumped into a tub beside the door.

Nash paddled his pirogue out between the trees and tied it up to the dock. Climbing out, he swung Marie up on his shoulders and started up the slope to the cabin.

'What kind of surprise you make for me?' she asked eagerly.

His smile widened. 'You'll see soon enough, *cher* Marie.'

They reached the front yard. It was littered with junk, most of which consisted of rusting auto parts. A pair of wooden swings hung from the branches of a cedar tree, and the dashboard of an old Ford F-1 pickup was propped against the covered porch, where it now served as a rough-and-ready child's toy.

Nash stopped before the cabin and set Marie down in front of him. Only now did she realize how strangely quiet her home was. Everything she normally associated with Honey Island — the hammering of red-bellied woodpeckers, the croaking of frogs and the ever-present buzz of the honeybees for which the swamp had been named — had stopped.

And where were her parents? Usually Papa would be working hard in the shed, skinning the nutrias and muskrats he trapped for a living, while Momma would be hanging washing or hoeing in their vegetable garden.

Now the place seemed to be abandoned.

Nash led her onto the garbage-strewn porch and opened the front door. With a soft creak, it swung slowly inward. Marie hesitated, suddenly uneasy, then stepped forward and peered into the gloom.

Instantly, she screamed.

She turned to run but Nash grabbed her. 'Non, non,' he hissed as she fought him, 'don't yell. I *hate* yellin'.'

But Marie didn't hear him. She had already retreated into a world of her own, driven to hysteria by what she'd just seen: by what Nash had done to her family.

Sobbing, tears running down her cheeks, she kept fighting him. He grabbed her wrists, thrust his face into hers and yelled: 'Stop it! Stop it, *cher* Marie, else

I'll have to hurt *you*, too!'

Still she lashed at him, jerking and twisting as she desperately tried to escape his grasp. Finally he back-handed her, stunning her so that she stumbled backward. Nash grabbed her before she fell and forced her to look into the cabin again.

'Look at them,' he said. 'They're beautiful, *oui*? No one hollering or arguing or fighting with each other. They just all seated around the table, quietly eating supper.'

'*Noooo* . . . ' she wailed.

'So quiet and peaceful,' Nash continued, his eyes glazing, his voice growing increasingly distant. 'No one angry with each other or — '

Marie suddenly sagged in his grip. It caught Nash off-guard. Instantly she twisted away from him, dodging his attempt to grab her as she ran.

Coming out of his reverie, Nash yelled, '*Come back!*' and chased after her. His long strides quickly gained on her. But as he got close and made another wild grab for her, he slipped, stumbled and fell to the ground.

'*Marie!*'

Onward she ran, a tiny, squealing figure with straggly fair hair flying wildly around her head. She made straight for his boat and Nash knew that if she reached it and got it untied, she might escape him altogether.

He could not let that happen.

Marie made it to the boat and frantically tried to free the mooring rope. But her little fingers couldn't untie the knot and before she was finished, Nash was upon her. Grabbing her by her long hair, he jerked her to her feet.

She fought him, screaming. 'Lemme go! Lemme go!' When he ignored her, she went limp, as she'd done before, but this time Nash wasn't buying it. He gripped her hair even tighter and let her scream.

'Momma! Papa! *Aidez-moi!*'

'They can't hear you,' Nash said. 'Not anymore.' He lifted her off the ground by her hair, making her scream even louder, and dragged her to the cabin.

There on the sunlit porch he tried to calm her. 'Now hush, *cher* Marie, hush. Be quiet and I will help you to see your

Momma and Papa again.'

He carried her into the cabin. It reeked of Watkins vanilla, garlic and blood.

Marie wept uncontrollably in his arms.

He set her down. Numb, she made no attempt to run. He ran his left forefinger down one blood-stained wall and then daubed the blood across each of her cheeks, transforming her into a bizarre-looking clown.

The touch of his finger tracing across her skin jerked her back to reality. She began screaming again. He tried to quiet her, but she ignored him and desperately fought to escape. One wild swipe caught his alligator-tooth necklace and tore it loose. Ivory fangs flew everywhere.

Nash straightened up, towering over her.

'That was *trés mal*, Marie,' he hissed softly.

Abruptly she froze and stared up at him.

She knew then, with sudden, unshakable certainty that he was going to punish her even worse than before.

She was right.

For several minutes the Gaspard family cabin was enveloped in silence. Then Nash came back out onto the porch.

Alone.

Ritualistically, he began to undress, carefully folding each item of clothing and placing it in a neat pile before removing the next.

Beneath his clothes, his naked body was daubed with three curious symbols, each one painted in dark, crusted blood.

Gaspard blood.

From his pants' pocket he took a pair of bloodstained latex gloves and a Smith & Wesson folding gut-hook knife. He thrust his hands into the gloves, flexed his fingers, and drew the short blade from its black handle.

Finally he put his head back and squinted at the sun, realizing by its position that he'd already been free for more than an hour and still had work to do before Ma discovered he was missing.

Then, with a faint smile, he walked slowly back into the cabin.

2

The thump-thumping of the helicopter's rotors as it hovered over the house made Kate Palmer stop varnishing the oak beam supporting her bedroom ceiling and, careful not to lose her balance, look out the window.

She couldn't understand what a chopper was doing way out here — a remote stretch of cliffs along the Virginia coast near the North Carolina state line — and set her brush down on the half-empty can of Old Spar varnish so that she could descend the ladder and find out.

She was a tall, lithe, refreshingly attractive woman. Just shy of thirty-eight, she had natural blonde hair cut in a boyish bob, unwavering amber eyes, a strong jaw and lips made for smiling. Lately, though, there hadn't been much to smile about.

Wiping her hands on her paint-smeared jeans, she put on her Rayban aviators and went out on the porch.

The chopper was descending now. Kate watched as it prepared to land on a patch of Wild Lupines growing between the tall, 112-year-old sandstone lighthouse and the rundown, two-story, clapboard keeper's house she now considered home. The downdraft from its whirling rotors flattened the neatly-mowed grass fronting the house and caused the rooster weather vane atop the chimney to spin wildly.

Dirt blew into Kate's face, forcing her to turn away — but not before she saw the FBI logo on the side of the helicopter.

As soon as the chopper touched down, a muscular young man of Puerto Rican descent jumped out. Except for the custom Tessori Uomo suits and exclusive Croata neckties he favored, he could have passed for a typical ponytailed, L.A. gang-banger. Ducked low, he ran toward her.

Kate smiled, delighted to have his company, for he was the closest thing she had to a true friend. Then, noticing the briefcase he carried, her pulse quickened.

Oh God, she thought. *Does this mean*

I've been reprieved? Or —

But the alternative didn't even bear thinking about.

★ ★ ★

After giving Special Agent Rosario 'Rosy' Ortiz a quick tour of the dilapidated house, Kate brewed a fresh pot of coffee and led him out on the porch facing the bleak, gray-green Atlantic.

They sat together on the rusty, creaking swing-seat, savoring the cool salty breeze while watching the seagulls lazily drifting on thermals overhead. Neither spoke. Neither seemed anxious to break the silence.

Finally Kate said: 'So — what do you think?'

'Awesome view,' he said.

'I meant the house.'

'Oh . . . it's . . . uh . . . great. Just great. Needs some TLC, maybe a little paint here and there, but other than that . . . ' He shrugged, not anxious to say what he really thought, and added lamely: 'I envy you.'

Kate laughed. 'You are such a liar. Even the real estate woman described it as a 'major fixer-upper.''

'But you bought it anyway?'

'Couldn't help myself. I've always wanted to live in a lighthouse. This was the next best thing.'

Rosy looked up at the historic structure but found no romance in it. 'Not me,' he said. 'I'm a city boy. Take me out of the mean streets and I turn into *calabazas rellenas.*'

Knowing he meant a pumpkin stuffed with cheese, Kate laughed again. One of the things she'd always liked about her partner was his ability to make her laugh. That was vital when you were two halves of a ViCAT — an FBI Violent Criminal Apprehension Team.

But she knew today he wasn't here for laughs; not in a Bureau helicopter.

Eager to know the reason, but at the same time worried that she might not like the answer, she glanced at the pilot. Back toward her, he stood at the edge of the cliffs, the collar of his windbreaker turned up against the stiff breeze, smoking as he

16

gazed out at the ocean.

'So,' she said, unable to stall any longer. 'Why don't you put me out of my misery?'

He did. 'You're back in, *jefe*,' he said carefully. '*If* you feel you're up to it.'

Relief surged through her and she felt almost lightheaded. 'Of course I'm up to it!' she breathed. 'I'm so fucking bored out here I'm going nuts!'

She might have said more, but suddenly all her pent-up emotions came rushing to the surface and she quickly turned away from him and let the tears flow.

He moved close, hesitated, and then put a comforting arm around her. It was difficult for him. Though they considered themselves partners, she'd been his boss for almost four years and he wanted it no other way. He loved his work, and knew he was damned good at it. But he had no interest in being the lead dog and from the first moment he and Kate had teamed up, he'd happily let her make all the final decisions. Now, here she was, this brilliant, sensitive, high-strung woman he so admired, weeping like a child, and it was on his shoulders to make things right for her.

'*Calmate*,' was all he could think to say.

'I don't want to calm down,' Kate said. 'I just want to get back to doing what I was born to do. Rat Man never should have put me out to pasture in the first place — '

'Whoa, whoa,' he said. 'The way I heard it, you could have avoided that by entering the Employee Assistance Program.'

'I didn't think I had a problem.'

'According to Rathman you developed dissociative tendencies and mild depersonalization — that sounds like a problem to me.'

She looked at him. 'Let's just forget it, right?'

'Let's just get one thing *straight* first,' he replied. 'What you do, boss, and how you do it . . . that takes a heavy toll. Doc Rathman asked you to enter the EAP under your own steam. You said no. He could have given you beach-time right there, and then your reputation would've been shot. But he didn't, and neither did Hayden. Instead they asked you — *asked* you — to take twelve weeks' unpaid leave to get your head together on your own time. What does that say to you?'

'You tell me.'

'Says they respect you and value you, boss, and that they want you back, ASAP. But they don't want you back at any price. They want you back only when you're ready for it.'

'I'm ready,' she said. But she wasn't completely sure about that. Only a few nights ago, she'd gotten out of bed before dawn and still in pajamas and robe, climbed to the top of the lighthouse. There she'd stood out on the platform, staring morbidly at the waves breaking on the rocks below, thinking how easy it would be to take a header and finish it once and for all.

But then a tiny voice in her head had reminded her that she'd been given a gift, a gift that ugly and painful as it could be at times, enabled her to do something helpful for humanity: to think like a serial killer, to get inside their heads and somehow guess correctly what they were thinking or planning to do next; to understand their twisted, often insane symbolism and then track them down and put them away before they could murder anyone else.

Feeling Rosy's eyes on her she said: 'Trust me. What have you got?'

'Let's go inside,' he said gently. 'I'll show you.'

They went back into the kitchen and Rosy took a manila envelope from his briefcase. From this he withdrew a series of stark scene-of-crime photographs which he set down on the table.

'I've got a fifty-one-fifty down in Louisiana,' he replied, using the police code for a violent-insane perpetrator. 'So far he's killed six people — all numbered here — ' he pointed to his forehead. 'He uses a short-bladed knife, a gut-hook, we think. He's a southpaw and he likes to kill up close and personal. No preferences — men, women, young, old. He ritualizes each kill, placing the bodies around the nearest table, and he takes their ears and tongues as trophies.'

'It's going to be a nightmare tracking him down,' she remarked. 'New Orleans is a big city.'

'He's not in the city. He's operating in the bayous about an hour's drive north east of New Orleans — place called Honey Island Swamp. He butchered a family of three a couple of months ago, but not thinking they were dealing with a serial killer the St Tammany Parish Sheriff's Office treated it as a random homicide. When he killed this second set of victims, they realized they were in over their heads and called for us.'

'When'd he kill the second set?'

'Twenty-two days ago.' Seeing her raised eyebrows, he said: 'Why do you think Hayden finally agreed to let you come back, *jefe*? No one's happy with the time it's taking to track this bastard down, least of all me.'

She picked up two photos depicting both murdered families. 'Husband, wife, wife's father for his opening act . . . a widow and two kids for an encore. Clues?'

'He leaves his fingerprints everywhere, albeit without meaning to. He wears latex gloves, but they're cheap, the kind you can buy at a supermarket or thrift store: too thin to fully disguise them.'

'I take it we haven't found a match?'

'Not yet.'

'Anything else?'

'He wears size ten boots. And there's something else that may or may not be relevant.'

'Which is . . . ?'

'Minute traces of alloy steels and zinc plating on the porch. So far the lab hasn't been able to link them to anything else on the property. Until they do, we've no idea where they came from. But if they're connected to the killer, they might be significant.'

She nodded. 'All right. Leave all this stuff with me. Where are you staying?'

'The Hampton Inn, Slidell,' he said, preparing to leave. 'I've established a temporary field office at Slidell PD.'

'Book me a room,' she said. 'I'll grab some things and join you there tomorrow.'

'There's something else you'll have to do first,' he said uncomfortably. 'Rathman wants to satisfy himself that you really are up to it before you start back.'

She pulled a face. 'So I have to go back to Quantico, take one of his long-winded examinations and wait a week for his evaluation? Our fifty-one-fifty could've murdered another six people by then.'

'It won't be that bad. Rathman's attending a conference at the Ritz-Carlton in Atlanta this week, so he'll be more or less on our doorstep. He'll see you tomorrow at one, then call Hayden with his evaluation. Whole thing won't take more than a day.'

Outside he signaled to the pilot that he was ready to leave. The pilot ground out his smoke, got into the 'copter and started the rotors whirling. Squinting in the downdraft Rosy turned back to Kate, hesitated, and then gave her an awkward kiss on the cheek.

'See ya, boss.'

Kate watched him duck low as he neared the whirling blades and then climbed in beside the pilot.

She waved a final time, then watched as the chopper lifted off, swung inland and flew away.

3

Twenty-four hours later Kate left her Chrysler rental with a valet parking attendant and entered the Ritz-Carlton Hotel with mixed feelings. The relief she'd felt at being reinstated had quickly given way to apprehension. After all, this thing wasn't cut and dried yet. Everything hinged on her being able to convince Dr Julius Rathman that she was mentally fit to return to work. If she couldn't do that, if for some reason he decided against allowing it . . .

Then she noticed the sign displayed prominently in the busy, tastefully-furnished lobby and her whole world seemed to tilt.

Renowned Neurosurgeon
ELLIOTT WARD
Will Be Signing His New Book,
SURGICAL SECRETS OF THE
PSYCHOPATHIC MIND
Today
Lecture in Mezzanine Conference Room

She stopped dead in her tracks. *Elliott?* Here?

At first she thought there must be some mistake, that this was *another* Elliott Ward. But there couldn't be two neurosurgeons with the same name.

She swallowed softly. Hardly a day went by that she didn't think about him, and yet she'd never, ever expected to see him again. She didn't have to see him now, of course. In fact, it was probably better if she didn't. And yet she couldn't deny her curiosity.

She glanced first at her watch, then up toward the mezzanine. She was still thirty minutes early for her appointment with Dr Rathman. And the thought of seeing Elliott again, even from a distance, was too strong to resist.

Ignoring the elevator she headed for the stairs, her heels clacking on the polished hardwood floor. This was probably a very bad idea. What did she hope to gain by seeing him again, anyway? Closure? On what, exactly? A relationship that had never existed anywhere outside her own adolescent imagination?

For a brief moment the urge to turn back was almost overwhelming, but she suppressed it. She'd never been a quitter and she wasn't about to start now. Besides, she was already carrying enough emotional scars as it was. There was no point in allowing this particular one to fester any longer. Deal with that and, she hoped, the others might start healing as well.

Doggedly she continued on up the stairs.

The softly-lit mezzanine had been decorated in a mixture of bold and pastel shades. A line of mostly chic older women were lined up to buy copies of the neurosurgeon's book from a perky young blonde who was on loan from his publisher. Gathered together near the adjoining conference room doors was a small group of reporters and cameramen.

Halting at the top of the stairs, Kate watched as one after another of Ward's admirers bought his book and then joined a second line, this one forming in front of a small desk at which Elliott himself would eventually sit, smile, sign and no doubt flirt notoriously. Kate frowned, wondering why that should bother her.

Just then the mezzanine filled with applause. She looked around and saw the conference room doors swing open and Elliott Ward emerge, surrounded by colleagues.

Her world tilted again.

He looked anything but a surgeon. But then, everything about him had always confounded expectation. Tall, tanned and athletic, he looked younger than his forty-five years. His face was long and narrow, with wide-set Prussian-blue eyes, a nose that was slightly snubbed and a rugged, square chin. His spiky hair was dark brown, finger-brushed carelessly back from his face and worn to collar-length. His cheeks were hollow, his thin mouth sober until he became aware of his adoring public. Then he turned on his bedside-manner smile, revealing white even teeth.

At first glance he looked like an internet billionaire, or maybe the way-ward son of a wealthy oil baron. But the truth was very different, and you could see it when you looked at his smooth, strong hands, with their long sensitive fingers. For here was a brilliant Manhattan neurosurgeon: quite possibly *the* most brilliant.

Immediately he was swamped by the awaiting press. A statuesque black reporter, accompanied by a cameraman, thrust a microphone into his face, saying: 'Veronica Baccus, WSB-TV. Doctor, just how much of your new book is speculation?'

'Deep Brain Stimulation isn't something I've just dreamed up, you know,' he said tolerantly. 'It's been around for more than a quarter of a century, and so there's a considerable body of evidence to prove its effectiveness. In patients suffering from Parkinson's Disease, for example, it can and does control tremor, rigidity, stiffness, slowed movement and balance issues. It also has useful applications for sufferers of dystonia, Multiple Sclerosis, epilepsy, essential tremor, Tourette's Syndrome and in some cases even severe depression. So there's very little reason to suppose that DBS can't also be employed to modify unacceptable or otherwise antisocial extremes of behavior.'

'Bradley Wagner, WDUN,' said a thin young journalist, pointing a Zoom H2 recorder in Elliott's direction. 'Just who qualifies for the surgery, doctor? The otherwise mild-mannered man who suddenly lashes out at his wife during an argument?'

'Of course not. If a man hits his wife, as unacceptable as that is, we can at least link it with an ascertainable motive — their original argument. But if that same man then decides to go off on a killing-spree, if he simply wants to kill or otherwise indulge his aggressive tendencies just for kicks ... well, who can ascertain the motive for that? *That's* the violence this procedure is intended to control, as much for the sake of the patient as the safety of the public.'

'But what gives us the right to change the way people behave?' Wagner persisted.

'If it's for the greater good and makes society a safer place in which to live, why not? The patient benefits from this as well, you know.'

A third reporter chimed in. 'Steven

Gadson, Associated Press. A lot of people are already saying that this is just lobotomy for the twenty-first century. How do you answer that?'

'For starters, the two procedures are completely different, the most obvious difference being that DBS is not destructive. It's adjustable and, if it fails to provide the required benefit, it's reversible. This isn't Frankenstein science we're discussing here, folks. This is keyhole surgery, minimally invasive, neat and effective.'

'So where will this neurotransmitter sit, exactly?' asked Gadson.

Elliott indicated his forehead. 'The frontal lobe is the center of highest intelligence and awareness. Around about here — ' he pointed to a spot a few inches above his left eye, ' — we have the hypothalamus, which among other functions, controls things like sex drive, anger and fear. The neurotransmitter, which is really little more than a set of wire-thin electrodes, would be implanted deep within the hypothalamus, then connected to what we call an IPG — an Implantable

Pulse Generator — placed under the skin about . . . here.' He indicated an area just below his left collarbone. 'But let's be absolutely clear about one thing. The purpose of the neurotransmitter is *not* to control the individual in whom it is fitted, but to control the aggressive, combative, sadistic or otherwise unacceptable extremes of antisocial behavior *within* that individual.'

'In the past, similar procedures have left patients with more problems than they started with,' said Baccus. 'Can you guarantee that this new procedure won't result in the same problems?'

'It's a cliché, I know, but by its very nature surgery — even relatively minor surgery — will always carry risks. However, the experiments we've already conducted on rats and pigs have given us no reason to suspect that there will be any unforeseen complications. Now, if you'll excuse me,' he said, 'I have some ladies waiting.'

As applause filled the mezzanine, Elliott made his way to the book-signing desk. Kate followed his every movement, her expression unreadable.

How *did* she feel, anyway, seeing him again after all these years? She hadn't really known what to expect and still wasn't sure, even now.

In the very next moment, however, all thought simply ceased.

She realized that he had spotted her in the crowd.

He stopped so quickly that he looked as if he'd walked into an invisible wall, his expression one of utter disbelief.

Knowing it was too late to run, Kate could only look back at him, trying to appear at ease. It was impossible. Around them, everyone, everything, every sound, seemed to vanish. And then he broke away from his entourage and came toward her, and the crowd parted before him like the Red Sea parting before Moses.

'Kate,' he said when he was close enough. 'My God, what — ?'

'It's been a while,' she managed. It was all she could think to say.

'Too long.' He fought to gather himself. 'What are you doing here? Do you live in Atlanta now?'

'Uh-uh. I'm here on business.'

'Will you be here for long?'

'I honestly don't know.'

'Perhaps I could call you later?'

'Well, I don't really — '

'Please,' he said.

Kate didn't know what to say.

Around them, Elliott's audience shifted awkwardly.

'Here,' he said, and quickly produced a business card. '*Please*,' he said again as he handed it to her. 'Call me.'

She took the card, swallowed and turned away. Her heart was pounding . . . and this time it had nothing to do with her imminent appointment with Rat Man.

4

It was still hot and muggy when Rosy parked his rental car on the sun-baked dirt fronting Leblanc's General Store & Bait Shop. A small, wood-framed eyesore with a rusty *Drink Jax Beer* sign above the door, it stood back from an old service road on a grassy bank overlooking the swamp.

As Rosy entered, he didn't hear the tiny chrome bell over the door tinkling as it had the first time he'd come here to question Leblanc about the Rivet killings. He looked up and noticed the bell was missing. Going to the refrigerated cabinet he helped himself to a Vernors and moved to the counter where the owner was sharpening a skinning knife on a whetstone. Popping open the can, Rosy took a long refreshing swig before asking: 'What happened to your bell?'

'I give it to a customer,' Jean Leblanc said. He was a heavyset old man who always wore flannel shirts and baggy denim overalls, and his white ponytail was longer than Rosy's. 'He be a good boy, but he's not so right in the head an' sometimes his mother, she wonder where he is.' He tested the blade on his thumb, spat on the whetstone and went on sharpening the knife. 'This way, she hears him comin' and goin'.'

'Good idea,' Rosy said.

'You ever catch that killer you was after, *m'sieur?*'

'Not yet. But you might be able to help me.'

'Doubt it. I answered all your questions last time.'

'Something's come up since then,' Rosy said. 'Do you stock latex gloves?'

Leblanc scowled sourly. 'Not no more.'

'But you did once?'

'While back, yeah.' He scowled again, as if angry with himself. 'Don't know why. Knowed from the get-go there wasn't no demand for 'em. Let myself get hooked by this hotshot salesman.'

'What happened to them?'

'I give 'em back. Lucky for me I took

'em on consignment. When nobody bought any, I called up the salesman an' he picked 'em up — all 'cept this one box which somehow got left behind.'

'Can I see it?'

'Ain't got it no more. It was in the storeroom for a time an' then it disappeared.'

Disappointed, Rosy said: 'Wouldn't happen to remember the brand, would you?'

Leblanc set his skinning knife down, took a ledger from under the cash register and thumbed through it. 'Gripp,' he said, indicating a page.

'Thanks.' Rosy scribbled the name in his notebook.

'Is it important?'

'Could be. You still got my card?' Rosy added.

'Right there in the register.'

'If those gloves ever show up, I'd appreciate it if you'd call me.'

'*C'est bon*,' Leblanc said.

'*Au revoir*,' Rosy said cheerfully and left.

★ ★ ★

Up in his fifth-floor suite at the Ritz-Carlton, Dr Julius Rathman, a thin, fastidious-looking man in his early sixties, with bristly white hair and omniscient brown eyes, said: 'First of all, Kate, let's get one thing clear. I'm not here to *judge* you, I'm here to *help* you. Believe it or not, I'm on your side.'

'Prove it,' she said.

'How?'

'Clear me to go back to work.'

'I'm not entirely convinced you're ready for that yet,' he replied. 'You're a fine agent, Kate. You possess an uncanny ability to climb inside a serial killer's head. But you pay a price for that. You immerse yourself in all these horrific killings day after day, twenty-four-seven, and you try to deal with it by simply filing it away in the back of your mind. Do you really think that's healthy?'

'What else am I supposed to do? Keep going through it over and over again until I really *do* fall apart?'

'You've *already* fallen apart, Kate. You just choose not to acknowledge it. And don't give me that look. Everything points to it. The last set of bloods we took show significantly raised plasma and salivary cortisol levels. How's your appetite?'

'Fine.'

'Well, it doesn't look like it. What did you weigh last month?'

'About one twenty-nine.'

'What do you weigh now?'

'I don't know.'

'A lot less than that.'

'So I've dropped a few pounds. Big deal.'

'How about panic attacks — had any recently?'

'No.'

'None?'

'Well, I wouldn't call them panic attacks.'

'What would you call them?'

'I wouldn't call them anything,' Kate said, trying to hide her anger. 'Okay, you're right. This can be a stressful job and sometimes . . . sometimes I overreact a little. Who doesn't?'

He didn't reply for a moment. Then he said: 'But you're still 'spacing out', aren't you? Still finding it hard to react emotionally the way you should. And making decisions ... that's still a nightmare, isn't it?'

'No.'

He smiled tolerantly. 'You know, Kate, the cure to almost any problem begins the same way. You have to admit that you have a problem. There's very little I or anyone can do while the patient is in denial.'

'I'm not *in* denial. I admit it. The job did start to get me down. And taking a break from it's been okay. But it's not the answer. I miss the job. It's me, it's what I am, what I do. You might just as well steal my identity from me.'

'So I tell Section Chief Hayden that you're cured, that it's okay for you to go back to work, and the first time you get up to your elbows in blood and guts you flip out completely, is that it?'

'No. For a start, I *don't* flip out. Never have.'

'It might be better for you if you *did*.'

Ignoring him, she said: 'The difference is, I now know where I've been going wrong, Doc. Ever since I joined the

Bureau all I've ever had, all I've ever wanted, is the job. Now I can see that maybe — probably — I should have balanced that with something else.'

'Like a family, you mean?'

'Possibly, but not necessarily. But definitely someone to share life with, someone to keep me grounded, give me a better perspective.'

'Got anyone in mind?'

She thought of Elliott, but only said: 'Still looking.'

'And what happens to you until he or she comes along?'

She smiled tiredly. 'The world's a messy place, Doc. All I want to do is restore a little order.'

'I wish you were as eager to restore order to your own life.'

'Take me away from the Bureau and I've got no order at all,' she said bitterly. 'Or life.'

Rathman mulled things over for a few moments, torn between his professional responsibilities and the fact that, as intractable as she could be, he liked her and knew she was an agent of exceptional

40

ability. At last he hefted his briefcase onto the coffee table between them and rummaged inside until he found his prescription pad. He scribbled something, then signed and handed her the completed script.

'Very well,' he said grudgingly. 'I'll go along with you — for now.'

Kate beamed. 'Mean I'm back on the job?'

'Effective immediately,' he confirmed. 'But in return you've got to do something for me.'

'Name it.'

'Have this filled the minute you get to Slidell — and *take* it.'

'What is it?' she asked, unable to read his scrawl.

'A combination of Lamotrigine and Prozac, twenty-five milligrams and twenty milligrams respectively.'

'I don't need an antidepressant — '

'I'm not prescribing it for depression, Kate. You don't realize it, but what ails you goes far deeper than that, and has potentially much more serious consequences. Now, this little cocktail isn't going to cure you by any means. But I believe it'll hold you together for the short term — until you let me really get to grips with curing you. Deal?'

'Deal,' she agreed, tucking the prescription into her purse.

'I *mean* this, Kate,' he warned. 'Not just as your shrink, but as your friend. You either give me your word that you'll start taking these pills today — and *stick* with them — or I will insist that Hayden find you a desk job for the rest of the year . . . maybe longer.'

'I promise,' Kate said. 'Cross my heart and hope to — '

'Don't say it, Agent Palmer,' Rathman said seriously. 'It's never a good idea to tempt fate.'

5

Elliott studied her above the rim of his vodka martini glass and said: 'Are you okay, Kate?'

It was almost an hour later and they were downstairs in the Atlanta Grill, seated in an intimate corner booth, enjoying drinks. The restaurant was richly lit and sensually opulent: surroundings that made it easy for her to forget the world outside and all the evils it contained.

'Sure,' she replied at last. 'Why? Don't I *look* okay?'

'Actually, you look a little thin. Tired.'

'Thanks.'

'I didn't mean it like that. Truth is,' he said, 'you look great. Better than great. Sensational.' He continued to admire her, and after a little said softly: 'God, it's good to see you again.'

She felt herself blushing and couldn't believe it.

At college Elliott had always been confident to the point of arrogance — and with good reason. He'd never really had to work at his studies. He seemed to have been blessed with an instinctive grasp of the concepts and practices of his chosen subject. And because everything always seemed to come so easy to him, so too did his complete and utter faith in himself.

In anyone else she would have considered such unshakable self-belief a turn-off. But in addition to his undoubted looks and intelligence, Elliott had something else going for him: an effortless ability to charm. And without even being aware of it, he had certainly charmed her.

By the time she realized that she was in love with him, he'd already been dating her best friend, Shannon Harper, for over a year. Worse, they were about to become engaged, and there was no way she could ever allow herself to come between them.

She thought again about how he had changed, not so much physically as emotionally, since she'd last seen him. Once so happy-go-lucky, there was an emptiness to him now that she should have foreseen but hadn't; and that made it even harder to hate him.

Hate.

Did he really deserve that? In the grand scheme of things, what he'd done to her hadn't been so terrible; especially since she had encouraged him. Truth was she couldn't even be sure why it still bothered her as much as it did. Perhaps it was because she had always considered Elliott as unfinished business. With him there had always been two unanswered questions. Had he really just used her back then? And if things *had* been different, could he have come to love her in the same way that she had loved — still loved — him?

His voice broke into her thoughts. 'I never told you this,' he was saying, 'but the night before I . . . we made love the first time — '

'The *only* time.'

'I came over to pick up Shannon and saw you toweling off by the window. I couldn't take my eyes off you.'

'You mean I was bare-ass?'

He nodded sheepishly.

'Jesus, Elliott! You — a Peeping Tom?'

'Well, I wouldn't go *that* far. But it made me horny as hell. I couldn't get you out of my mind all night. And the next day, when I came by . . . ' He didn't finish. He didn't need to. By her expression he knew the memory was as vivid to her as it was to him.

But almost immediately reality intruded. 'What's wrong?' he asked, seeing her troubled frown.

'Nothing,' she said. 'Everything. I'm sorry, Elliott. I was wrong to gatecrash your life again.'

He grinned. 'Do you hear me complaining?'

★ ★ ★

They were just getting ready to eat lunch when the maitre d' brought a young girl to their booth. She was about fourteen, with a pale, heart-shaped face framed by side-parted butter-colored hair texture-cut to just above the shoulder.

'Chelsea!' Elliott rose to greet the

newcomer. 'Here, sit down, honey. I want you to meet an old friend of mine, Kate Palmer. Kate, my daughter, Chelsea.'

Kate offered her hand. 'Hi, Chelsea.'

'Hey,' Chelsea said listlessly.

'What'll you have, sweetheart?' Elliott asked.

'Nothing. I'm not hungry.'

'You must be.'

'I'm not.'

'How about the toasted vegetable wrap?'

She shrugged. 'Whatever.'

She wore a tight black tank top, slim-leg jeans and an expensive pair of Baby Phat Diva trainers. She was slim and already attractive, with unusually pale green eyes and freckled cheeks, but her sulkiness and slouchy body language destroyed some of her appeal.

There was an awkward silence.

Finally Kate said: 'My God, talk about the apple not falling far from the tree. You could be a carbon copy of your mother.'

Chelsea perked up, as Kate had hoped. 'You knew my mom?'

'Uh-huh.' Kate glanced at Elliott, held

his gaze a moment, then turned back to Chelsea. 'We were roommates in college. Best friends.'

'Did you know she was killed?'

'In a car accident, yes. I'm so sorry.'

'We've managed to pull through it,' Elliott said. He squeezed his daughter's hand. 'Right, sweetheart?'

'If you say so.'

There was another awkward silence.

Kate said: 'So, how're you enjoying the tour? Must be exciting, flying around the country with your dad?'

'It's okay, I guess.'

Elliott rolled his eyes. 'Jeez, Chels', don't die of excitement. She wanted to go waterskiing with some friends,' he explained to Kate, 'but I made her come with me.'

'Which would *you* rather do?' Chelsea asked Kate.

'Don't answer till you hear my side,' said Elliott.

He was only joking, but Chelsea didn't take it that way. 'That's the trouble,' she said bitterly. 'It's always *your* side. You pretend that what I say is important, but it isn't. Not really. All you care about is being in control.'

'Honey, that's not true.'

'Then why am I here?'

'We've already been through this a dozen times.'

'Yeah, always from your point of view.'

'That's enough,' Elliott said. 'Let it go.'

'See?' Chelsea said to Kate. 'This is what always happens. He asks for my opinion and then shuts me up before I can give it.'

'I said that's enough!' Elliott snapped.

Chelsea promptly got up.

'Where're you going?'

'Back to the room.'

'Chelsea, wait — '

She ignored him and hurried out of the restaurant.

Watching her go, Elliott sighed wearily. 'As you can see, Tweedledum and Tweedledee we ain't.'

'Tweedledee was never a teenager.'

'You think that's what's at the heart of it?'

'That'd be my guess. It's been a while, but I still remember my own raging

49

hormones. All you can do is hang in there and be patient. She'll get over it.'

'I wish I shared your optimism. Ever since Shannon died I've been Public Enemy Number One, and I don't like it.'

'Trust me, Elliott, it's no picnic for her, either.'

Their food arrived. Both had ordered the Oriental chicken salad. It looked delicious, but Kate just picked at hers.

'Now I see why you're so slim,' he said.

'Will you stop going on about my weight?'

'I've only mentioned it twice. That's not 'going on'.'

'All right, all right. Here, look.' She forked a piece of chicken into her mouth and chewed with exaggerated relish. 'Hmmm. Yummy. Happy now?'

'I'm happy you're *here*.'

'So am I, God help me.'

Reaching for his wine glass, he eyed her thoughtfully. Then the frustration that had been simmering inside him ever since their first meeting finally boiled over. 'How could you just run off like that?' he demanded, trying to keep his voice low.

'Do you know how much we missed you? How many times Shannon and I wondered where you were, if you were okay?'

Kate sat back, what little appetite she'd had suddenly gone. 'It was a shitty thing to do, I admit. But at the time I couldn't help myself.'

'I was sure you'd call when Shannon died.'

'I wanted to . . . God knows how many times.'

'But . . . ?'

'Do I have to spell it out for you?'

'We made a mistake,' he said.

'Oh, is *that* what it was?' she said angrily. 'Well, if you'd only told me that at the time it would've explained *everything*.'

'What was there to explain?'

'For starters: why you went out of your way to pretend that nothing ever happened between us — and that I'd somehow ceased to exist.'

He looked away. 'All right, that makes us even. *You* did a shitty thing. I did a shitty thing. But I had my reasons, believe me.'

'I'd really love to hear them.'

Before he could reply, however, her cell phone buzzed. She checked the caller ID, saw it was Rosy and said: 'Talk to me.'

Rosy said: 'We've got three more, boss. Same M.O. and . . . ' He continued to talk but his voice kept fading in and out.

'Speak up, Rosy. I'm losing you,' Kate said. 'What'd you say?'

'Hard to get a signal out here in the swamp,' he explained. 'I said it's the same M.O., including the numbers carved on the victims' foreheads.'

'When did it happen?'

'M.E. puts it at a little over twenty-four hours ago.'

'Okay, I need to get there ASAP. Line up a Bubird for me,' she said, using Bureau-speak for the FBI's fleet of aircraft.

'I'm way ahead of you, boss. But there's nothing available at the moment, so I've gone private. There's a Hawker 400 waiting for you at DeKalb-Peachtree. It'll get you here in about an hour.'

As she stuffed the phone back into her

purse she said: 'I'm sorry, Elliott, but I have to go.'

'I was hoping we could have dinner tonight.'

'Maybe next time.'

'You're not pulling another vanishing act on me?'

'No. But I really do need to go.'

'Problems at work?' he asked. Then when she didn't answer: 'Just what are you these days, anyway — a lawyer?'

'Uh-uh. I'm with the FBI.'

'You're a *Fed?*'

'Who'd have thunk it, right?'

Elliott smiled. 'I'm impressed. Are you on a case right now? I mean, is that what brought you to Atlanta?'

'Sorry. I can't discuss that.'

'Not even a hint?'

She hesitated, then said: 'Ever hear of VICAP?'

'Sure. Violent Criminal Apprehension Program. It's an FBI data information center. I mentioned it in my book. Deals with serial killers and sexual homi — ' He broke off as something hit him. 'Wait a minute. Are you saying there's another

Ted Bundy running around in New Orleans?'

'Of course not.'

'Don't lie to me, Kate. We'll be in New Orleans day after tomorrow, and I've got Chelsea to consider.'

She stalled, wondering how much she could tell him, then said: 'You didn't hear this from me, okay?'

'Sure.'

'Our 'problem' isn't in the city. It's in the bayous about twenty miles northeast.'

6

In the bayous, about twenty miles northeast . . .

The old tree-house nestled unevenly in the spreading branches of a squat, thick-boled cypress. In this remote corner of the swamp, it had lain derelict and overgrown for so long that few people even remembered it was still there. Perched twelve feet off the ground, it tilted at a slight angle and was covered with vines and tree orchids. Its corrugated iron roof was now red with rust.

The only way it could be reached was by an old, moss-covered rope ladder dangling from a narrow leaf-strewn porch. Many of the ladder's rungs were missing and those that remained looked unsafe. The front door hung lopsidedly from one hinge and at the rear of the structure a small tarpaper window over-looked a stagnant, weed-filled pond. Known as Peetre's Pond, it tapered at the far end into a brush-choked neck of shallow water that connected it to the creek beyond.

Inside the tree-house, a small hand-made table and chair sat in the middle of the dirt-covered floor. An old sack curtain had long-since mildewed and fallen from the window, while curled beside it on the floor was a length of knotted rope. The rusty meat-hook at one end suggested that the rope was an emergency exit in case the ladder ever broke.

The eerie quiet of the hovel was suddenly broken by an uneven creaking sound. Someone was climbing the ladder, moving with great caution. Their ascent made the branches tremble and the tree-house groan like a slowly-sinking ship.

Moments later the broken door creaked open and a long, thin shadow stretched across the floor. Its owner followed it inside and closed the door behind him. He looked around and shook his head in sad wonderment. Everything was exactly as he remembered it. And so it should be. In what seemed like another lifetime he'd built this place for his two sons.

He dropped his bag to the floor. The moldy dust of more than a decade puffed up around it. He looked about him, absorbing his surroundings, and then carefully sat in the chair. It creaked beneath him but didn't collapse. He wearily rested his elbows on the table and once more looked around. Hell, he thought, he'd done nothing more than swap one prison cell for another. But he hadn't known where else to go. This place had always been a retreat, for him as much as the boys. Why shouldn't he retreat here now, at least until he got back on his feet?

It had been a hell of a day, the first day of freedom he'd known in fifteen years, and it had left him physically and emotionally drained. He closed his eyes, his head still reeling from everything he'd had to absorb, especially the conditions of his parole, which were many.

They'd granted him his freedom but they expected him to live by more rules now than he ever had in prison. But maybe that was no bad thing. The system had emasculated him. And yet he was definitely a better man for it. Back then he'd been a mean-spirited, quick-tempered, brutal son of a bitch ready to steal, fight, and get drunk whenever the mood took him.

Though he did not believe it at the time, the courses he'd been forced to attend in prison eventually taught him to be a better man. Skeptical at first, he'd eventually learned to manage his anger and understand his emotions, to solve problems, step back and adopt a more measured approach to life-events. But in so doing he'd also learned to think more deeply than before and he didn't always like the ugly, painful thoughts that occupied his mind — like not being there for his sons when they needed him most.

Opening his bag he took out a cardboard folder containing some paint-ings he'd done in his cell. Wiping the table clean with his sleeve, he carefully spread them out. They were all similar looking. In vivid colors, they depicted Egyptian-styled glyphs and symbols arranged in a seemingly haphazard fashion around a central, stylized pharaoh figure. Each pharaoh wore a ceremonial robe with an elaborate, beaded collar, and an ornate crocodile-shaped *nemes*, or headdress. All the symbols, including the snakes and birds, faced inward, as if paying homage to the pharaoh, who looked off to the side. And though his face was in profile there was no mistaking the resemblance of one image to the man seated at the table.

He gazed fondly at the paintings, as if drawing spiritual comfort from them. Now if only his precious books were here, he thought, the day would be perfect. But they weren't, and for the moment all he had to occupy him was his memories, the good and the not-so-good.

7

Rosy was waiting at the passenger gate when Kate touched down at Slidell Municipal Airport a little under an hour later.

'What've you got for me, *hombre?*' she asked.

They fell into step, heading for the exit to the parking lot. 'The Gaspard family,' he replied. 'Clovis Gaspard, age 32, Valérie Gaspard, 28, daughter Marie, age eight. All stabbed to death, all with their ears and tongues removed.'

'And this happened about noon yesterday?'

'That's the M.E.'s guesstimate.' They reached his rental car. Rosy slid in behind the wheel while Kate rode shotgun. 'We'll have a better idea when she opens them up.'

'Witnesses?'

'We should be so lucky.'

'But they're numbered?'

'Seven through nine.'

There was something in his tone that made her look at him and see for the first time just how troubled he'd been all along. 'Bad?' she asked softly.

He gave a despondent shrug. 'Let's just say our boy's getting more and more creative.'

They drove south along Airport Road and turned left onto I-12E. 'How was your meeting with Rathman?'

'It's official,' she said. 'I'm back.'

Rosy grinned, his teeth strong and white against his coffee-colored skin. 'Man, that's great!'

She shared his enthusiasm, but only to an extent. As they took exit 83 for US-11 she suddenly became aware that her entire career, everything she'd fought so hard to achieve, was riding on this case. Fuck up now and she could kiss her dreams goodbye — not to mention her pension. The Bureau needed agents, not liabilities, and for all her talk to the contrary, she still wasn't completely sure which one she was anymore.

About twenty minutes later they

reached Crawford's Landing. A tall, hard-bellied, unyielding man in a gray, button-down uniform shirt, matching pants and a black tie stood hipshot on the dock, watching them approach.

Rosy said: 'That's our liaison with the St Tammany County Sheriff's Office. Deputy Donald Doucet. He can be a hard-nosed SOB at times but he's a stand-up guy, and he knows his turf.'

They parked, got out and crossed the lot to Deputy Doucet. As she got closer, Kate saw that he was in his early fifties, with a time-worn face and cool slate-gray eyes. She extended her hand and he shook it roughly.

'Special Agent Palmer?' he said curtly.

'Correct.'

'Well, I hope you know what you're up against here.'

'I've been fully briefed.'

'Good. Because you got a lot to prove.' He gestured toward the 16-foot white skiff moored behind him and said: 'Let's go.'

★ ★ ★

As Slidell fell behind them and the vast foreboding swamp opened up ahead, Kate slapped away a swarm of black flies and turned to the deputy. 'Who found the bodies?'

'I did.'

'Were you tipped off?'

'No. Like I told your partner, I like to make a routine sweep every day or two, 'specially since the murders started. When I reached the Gaspard place I knew something was wrong. Clovis Gaspard trapped and skinned muskrats for a living. You'd always find him working outside his shed. But there was no sign of him. The house was quiet, the front door wide open.'

'And when you went ashore . . . ?'

'You could smell it. The blood, I mean. Kind of coppery, like acid rain. And when I got closer I heard the flies.' He drew a breath. 'Anyway, I secured the scene, called the M.E. and you folks.'

Twenty minutes later Doucet indicated ahead and said: 'We're here.'

Kate and Rosy turned and saw the Gaspard house on a small grassy shoal in front of them. Doucet killed the motor and shifted the tiller, sending the boat gliding toward the dilapidated dock.

The boat bumped gently against the old tires protecting the pilings. Doucet jumped out and tied up next to a 19-foot aluminum Jon boat. Aboard it a medical crew sat drinking coffee while waiting for Kate's permission to remove the bodies to the St Tammany Parish Coroner's Office. Nearby, four pirogues had been dragged up onto the shoal by the CSI team.

Accompanied by Deputy Doucet, Kate and Rosy climbed the slope to the Gaspard cabin. Yellow POLICE LINE DO NOT CROSS tape fluttered in the dank humid breeze, marking off a single exit and entryway and a safe area where personnel could confer without fear of contaminating evidence. Lab agents in white coveralls were still dusting, photo-graphing and logging everything that looked unusual or out-of-place, and a zone search was in progress.

Kate and the others stopped at the police tape that prevented entrance to the cabin. 'Hey, Les,' Deputy Doucet called. 'FBI's here.'

Almost immediately a wiry, balding little man in coveralls appeared in the doorway. Nodding hello to Deputy Doucet, he lifted the tape for them to duck under. Kate flashed her I.D. and introduced herself and Rosy.

'I'm Les Fields, Senior CSI, St Tammany Parish Sheriff's Office,' the little man said. 'Welcome aboard.' He wiped his rimless glasses on one blood-stained sleeve.

'What have we got so far?' she asked.

'A slaughterhouse,' he replied.

'Prints?'

'Everywhere, even though he's still wearing gloves. The same pair, actually.'

'Oh?'

Fields nodded. 'Sure. Even a good-quality latex glove will develop a print pattern if you wear it often enough.'

'Anything else?'

'Plenty of boot-prints, size ten. Pretty standard sole, so don't hold your breath. Oh, and we've got this.'

He held up a plastic evidence bag containing a yellowish, conical-shaped tooth.

Kate peered at it. 'Alligator?'

'Uh-huh.' He held the bag close to her face. 'You can see where it's been drilled,' he said. 'I'm thinking it was part of a necklace. They're fairly common around here.'

'So it's possible there was a struggle and the necklace broke.'

'That'd be my guess.'

'Which means the tooth could be anybody's.'

'Yes and no. It's the only tooth we found. To me, that suggests it belonged to the killer. Otherwise, why would he have wasted time picking up all the other teeth?'

'Where did you find this one?' Rosy said.

'On the floor just inside the front door. He must've missed it, or not bothered to count how many teeth he had.'

'Okay if we look around inside?' Kate asked.

'Help yourself. Everything's still in situ.' Stepping aside so they could enter the cabin, he added: 'But brace yourself, Agent Palmer. It ain't pretty.'

Before she could move, Doucet caught Kate's arm. 'I got work to do,' he said. 'Have fun.'

He hurried off before she could reply.

8

For almost as long as she could remember, Ma Guidry — a short, hulking, overweight woman squeezed into a threadbare floral-print dress and scuffed, square-toed shoes — had felt old beyond her years. Sow-faced and puffy-eyed, her mouth crowded into a small, vacant space between her heavy jowls, she had in her lifetime been plagued by everything from hypertension and joint pain to diabetes and breathing difficulties.

But to her credit, she had never complained about her infirmities. As far as she was concerned they were punishments from God, and she deserved every one of them. The idea that God may in fact have been punishing the *wrong* Guidry all this time never occurred to her, for Ma was devout in her beliefs and knew that God never made mistakes.

It had been so long since Ma had

enjoyed good health that she could no longer remember what it felt like. These days it was all she could do to roll out of bed just before sunrise, tie on her old wraparound dress and then lumber down through the gloomy weatherboard and shingle house to the old, worn sofa on the porch, where she spent her days watching the murky waters of Middle Creek move sluggishly by.

It was now the middle of the afternoon. Sunlight sparkled pleasantly off the olive-brown water, while green-and-gold dragonflies skimmed the surface, hunting insects. Ma sat on the sofa cleaning mudbugs.

Occasionally she looked toward Noah, who was hunkered down at the far end of the dock, doing his clumsy best to repair some loose boards. His every movement made the tiny chrome bell pinned to his coveralls tinkle. It wasn't a loud tinkling, but Ma could hear it when he was working in or around the house and she was grateful to Jean Leblanc for giving it to him.

Whenever her eyes settled on him, her

face clouded. Though she wasn't even yet fifty, her health was beginning to deteriorate faster than ever, and she had no idea what would happen to her boys once she was gone.

Nash and Noah, she thought: identical mirror twins, opposites in every way, including their blue and blue-gray eyes. They were as different in personality and temperament as night and day. Noah was gentle, kind and slow-witted, a six-year-old in a man's body. Nash was the exact opposite: cruel, spiteful and manipulative. But both had one thing in common: they were misfits with no place in this world, and without their mother to continue guiding them through life, she hated to think what would become of them.

She watched Noah hammering a nail into one of the new boards. He struck it slantwise and it buckled. Dismayed, he wrenched the nail out, added it to the pile of bent nails beside him and tried again. He'd been doing that for the past ten minutes.

The whine of an outboard motor suddenly caught his attention. He stopped hammering and eagerly looked toward the sound. Ma did the same. Shortly, a white skiff appeared out of the swamp, leaving a v-shaped wake of ripples as it approached the dock.

Although Ma's eyesight was failing, she recognized Deputy Doucet seated at the stern.

As Doucet got closer, the house and the white satellite dish through which Ma received her TV reception, the dock and Ma's vintage blue VW Westfalia camper parked beside the woodshed were all reflected clearly in his mirror-sunglasses.

Nearing the dock, he cut the engine and tossed Noah a rope. Noah made a fumbling catch with both hands, almost dropping it, and then managed to concentrate hard enough to tie up the skiff.

''Afternoon, Noah,' Doucet climbed onto the dock, removed his cap and used his forearm to wipe the sweat from his forehead. 'Hot one, ain't it?'

'Hidee, sheriff! *Oui, oui*, it surely is hot awright. Hot as a . . . ' he paused, unable to think of an analogy. Then, embarrassed,

71

he looked away, avoiding eye contact, his demeanor meek and subservient. 'Gonna stay for supper? I catched plenty crawfish! Ma's cleaning 'em right now.'

'Thanks, son. Maybe next time.'

Seeing Noah's disappointment, Doucet reached into his pocket. 'But I did fetch you some candy,' he said. He handed Noah the red-and-purple box of Bottle Caps he'd bought for himself that morning, before he'd found the Gaspards and heaved his breakfast. 'I know you got a sweet tooth.'

Noah's eyes bugged with joy. '*Candi!*' He waved the box excitedly. 'Ma, Ma, look what the sheriff brung me!'

Popping one of the cherry-flavored candies into his mouth, he skipped alongside the deputy, his little bell tinkling with each step. Together they climbed up the steep dirt slope to the Guidry front porch.

The deputy stopped respectfully at the foot of the porch steps, removed his cap and fanned himself with it. As she continued to spray-clean the crawfish, then pull their heads off, Ma said: 'Hope you ain't here to blame one of my boys for somethin', 'cause Nash don't live here no more, and Noah, he ain't been out of my sight all week.'

'Not here about your boys, Ma.'

Relieved, she stopped cleaning the crawfish, set the bucket aside and turned to Noah. 'Go get the Deputy some lemonade, son. An' don't spill it all 'fore you get back.'

Noah shook his head fervently. 'I won't, Ma. Promise. You'll see. I do it just as good as Nash would. Nash never spills *nothin*',' he confided to Doucet.

The lawman smiled tolerantly and watched Noah shamble up onto the porch and into the house. 'Boy sure does idolize his brother, don't he?'

'Always been that way,' said Ma. 'He'd do anythin' to please Nash, an' Nash knows it.' She slapped away a persistent gallinipper and gestured to the other end of the sofa. 'Take the weight off. Cooler up here.'

'Obliged.'

'Lot of folks think God cheated me with Noah,' Ma continued as the Deputy flopped down. 'But he'll do anythin' you ask and don't have a mean bone in him. Good Lord just forgot to give him all the parts.'

'I guess He was too busy giving 'em to Nash,' Doucet said before he could stop himself.

Ma's sharp, steely glance made him add quickly: 'Oh, I ain't knockin' the boy. But he sure does make a body feel uncomfortable.'

'That's 'cause he's so smart. Don't you know the smart ones always make you feel uncomfortable?'

Deputy Doucet nodded. That was an understatement. Though he hadn't seen Nash for years, he could still remember the way the boy had always looked at him, as if he were a lowly bug that needed squashing.

The door opened and Noah rejoined them. He held a fruit jar full of lemonade in both hands, staring fixedly at it, his tongue touching the corner of his mouth in concentration.

'I didn't spill none, Ma,' he said after he'd given the makeshift glass to the deputy. 'I didn't, honest. I done it just like Nash would.'

'Can see that, son,' said Deputy Doucet, taking a long appreciative gulp. 'That sure is good, Ma.'

Unable to contain herself any longer, she said gruffly: 'When you gonna tell me why you here?'

The deputy hesitated, then said: 'If you see any strangers, no matter how friendly they seem, keep your distance, Ma.'

'I'll be sure to do that.' Ma snapped her fingers at Noah, who was now sitting slouched over on the top step, rocking back and forth like a hyperactive child. 'You hear that, son? No talkin' to strangers.'

'Sure, Ma, sure. I heard. No talkin' to strangers. I can remember that.'

'An' keep that old .45 of yours handy,' Doucet added. 'I don't want you two ending up like the Gaspards.'

'Somethin' bad happen to 'em?' Noah asked anxiously. 'Huh? Huh?'

'Very bad, son. They've all been murdered.'

Noah's eyes bugged and he buried his

face in his big-knuckled hands.

'*Mon Dieu*, no!' Ma breathed. 'Who'd do such a sinful thing?'

'Dunno. But we found a 'gator tooth by the door in their cabin.'

Ma looked uneasy. 'Wouldn't be the first time *le cocodrie* attack' folks in their own homes.'

'No 'gator did this,' Doucet said grimly. 'Not unless it knew how to use a real sharp knife. 'Sides, the tooth had a hole drilled through it, like it come from a necklace.'

Noah looked up. 'Ma — '

'Get inside, son,' she said quickly.

'But Ma — '

'Get inside, or I'll take the whip to you!'

Noah rose slowly, fighting tears, and shuffled back inside.

Once he'd gone, Ma turned angrily to the deputy. 'Shouldn't talk like that in front of him. He ain't got the stomach for it, him still bein' a child an' all.'

'Sorry, I wasn't thinkin'.' Deputy Doucet set his empty fruit jar down. 'Thanks for the lemonade, Ma.' Rising, he hitched up his pants and said, almost as an afterthought: 'Peyton got out of prison today. You know that, right?'

'I got it marked on my calendar,' she said.

'Well, if you see him — '

'I won't.'

'If you see him,' he continued patiently, 'tell him he's got forty-eight hours to contact his nearest probation office. That's in Covington. Okay?'

'*Oui*,' she said. 'But I won't be seein' him.' She said it more as if she were trying to convince herself.

Deputy Doucet flicked a bug from his shirt, squared his hat on his head and plodded down the slope to the dock.

As Ma started cleaning the crawfish again, Noah reappeared in the doorway.

'Ma?'

'Not now, son.'

'But Ma, I got to tell you somethin'.'

'What?'

'I already forgot. What you told me not to forget.'

'Don't talk to strangers,' she repeated, never taking her eyes from Deputy

77

Doucet's broad back.

'Sure,' said Noah. 'I remember now. Don't talk to strangers. I can remember that.'

But she knew that he couldn't, leastways not for any length of time.

9

As soon as Deputy Doucet was gone, Ma told Noah to help her up from the porch sofa. Wheezing from the effort, she lumbered indoors. Each painful step made her wince. Crossing to the living room coffee table, she knelt down on one swollen knee.

Noah watched her anxiously from the door.

Ma groped around under the table. Nothing. Praying she was mistaken, she tried again. Still nothing. Her worst fears realized, she straightened up and glared at Noah. 'So you helped him, did you?'

Too afraid to answer, Noah whimpered.

Ma stormed past him to the stairs. 'Come with me, boy.'

'Aw, Ma, do I have to? Huh. Huh?'

''Less'n you want a taste of the whip?'

He shook his head and eyes lowered, obeyed her.

As Ma labored upward, she looked

toward the shadowy bedroom doors and thought: *How could you, boy? Dear God, how could you?*

At the top of the stairs she grabbed her husband's old bullwhip from a hall closet.

Noah panicked. 'N-No, Ma, don't. Don't. Don't whip him.'

'*Bouche ta guile!*' she said. 'Or you'll be next.'

Noah shut up.

★   ★   ★

The rusty fan whirring on the window sill buffeted the flies about but did nothing to lessen the intense, humid heat.

Sweating, Nash Guidry lay on his bed reading a decades-old English-language translation of the *Book of the Dead*. The paperback was soiled and creased from constant usage and its pages had long ago turned brown. But he treated it lovingly, and every now and then he stopped reading and gently ran his finger over the legend neatly printed inside the front cover:

Property of P. Guidry.

Nash had found the book years ago while he was exploring the attic. It was one of many belonging to his father.

His room — a glorified cell in which his mother had kept him confined since he was nineteen — contained an old bed, table with a lamp, a straight-backed chair, a closet and a chest of drawers on which sat a bowl and pitcher. A plastic bucket in the corner served as a toilet.

Setting the book down, he stretched the stiffness from his back. He then swung his legs over the bed, the chain padlocked around his right ankle clanking on the floor.

The chain was anchored to the floorboards. It allowed him to go only as far as the chalk line Ma had drawn on the floor or the barred window opposite the door. He lived, slept, ate, plotted, fantasized and hated within these four walls, and always he dreamed of being free.

Over the years he'd tried numerous ways to escape, from fashioning skeleton keys out of empty Coke cans to trying to unscrew the bolts in the ground anchor, but nothing had worked. Not even pestering Noah to look for Ma's spare key. Nash knew she must have hidden it somewhere, in case she ever lost the one on the shoelace around her neck. But Noah had never found it.

Until two months ago. Then, while searching under the furniture for his pet turtle, Pookie, he'd found the spare key taped under the coffee table. From then on Nash had been free to turn his murderous fantasies into reality.

At first, he'd considered running away. But then he'd realized that he was safer at home. There, by pretending to be chained up in his room, he had the perfect alibi. All he had to do was never let Ma know he could escape. So after every foray into the swamps he always made Noah put the key back where he'd found —

The door burst open, startling him. He looked up and saw Ma wedged in the doorway, Noah peering anxiously over her shoulder.

'Put the book down!' she wheezed.

Nash grudgingly obeyed. The whip in his mother's hand told him why she was here, but he showed no fear.

'Now give me that damned key!' she snapped.

'What key?'

'Don't play games, boy. The key Noah give you to get free.'

'What're you talking about?' He rattled his chain at her. 'Does it look like I'm free?'

'You're askin' for a thrashin', boy.'

'I'm tellin' you the truth.' He gestured about him. 'Go ahead. Look around. You can wear your knees out, but you still won't find no key.'

Ma lumbered into the room, the floorboards creaking underfoot. But she was careful not to cross the chalk line on the floor. Any closer and she would be within Nash's reach.

Nash retreated into the corner but refused to cower. 'You got the only key, Ma. It's around your neck!'

'It's the spare I want,' she said. 'Somehow you got your brother to find it an' give it to you.'

Nash glared at Noah. 'If he told you that, he's a liar.'

'Nah, it's the only way it could've

happened,' she raged. 'I spawned you like Eve spawned Cain and I'll always love you, no matter what. But as God is my holy witness, boy, I'll never understand you. The Gaspards were like kin. We broke bread together, prayed together — '

'Get off your pulpit,' Nash sneered. 'The Gaspards were nothing but inbred swamp rats. Whoever killed 'em did everyone a favor.'

'May the Lord strike you dead for that.' Ma shook out the whip, ready to strike, but Noah grabbed her arm.

'No, Ma, don't! Don't whip him. *Please!*'

She jerked her arm free and glared at Nash. 'You can't wriggle out of this, boy! The law ain't stupid. The deputy says they found a 'gator tooth in their cabin. Had a hole drilled in it, just like the ones on your necklace.'

'So what? Plenty of folks have necklaces like mine. Bracelets, too.'

'But none of them is the child of *Satan!*'

'Ma,' he said, 'if I'd gotten loose, you think I'd come back here so you could keep hollerin' and whipping me? Hell, I'd be gone so fast my shadow couldn't keep up with me!'

Ma snapped her whip, making both sons flinch. 'For the last time, boy,' she rasped, 'you gonna give me that key or do I whip it out of you?'

'Go ahead,' Nash said. 'Whip all you want. I don't have your goddamn key!'

'I . . . I got it,' Noah blurted.

Silence draped the room as he dug a key out of the bib-pocket of his coveralls and held it up before Nash could stop him.

'See, see, I ain't lyin'. I got it. I got the key. I'm sorry,' he said to Nash. ''S'all my fault. I forgot to put it back after you give it to me.' He started crying.

Ma felt sick. The other murders, the Clemenceaus and the Rivets . . . she'd persuaded herself that Nash couldn't have done them. He was safely locked away. Just to make sure, after both crimes she'd gone to the coffee table with her heart in her mouth, felt around until she touched the key and then sighed with relief. But now . . .

She looked at the whip. What good

would a whipping do now? The damage had already been done. Nine lives taken . . .

Her mind spun; she could barely breathe. She knew she had to sit down before she collapsed. Snatching the key from Noah, she hurried from the room.

Nash turned from the window and glared at his twin. 'You dumb fuck,' he said.

Noah cried even harder. His sobs blurred his words. Over and over he repeated how sorry he was, how he didn't mean it and it would never happen again. Nash let him blubber on. He needed time for his rage to subside.

'P-Please, Nash, say you forgive me. I didn't mean it. Honest to God. I . . . I . . . just forgot. I won't never do it again. I swear. Next time I'll remember. I promise.'

'There won't *be* a next time, you moron!'

Noah wailed and sank to the floor.

Nash ignored him. But when Noah continued to wail, he crossed the room as far as the chain would stretch and growled irritably: 'All right, all right, quit bawlin', damn you. I forgive you.'

Sniffing back his tears, Noah forced himself to meet his brother's gaze. ''Mean y-you ain't mad at me no more?'

'Uh-uh.'

'Y'sure? Huh? Huh?'

'Yes-I'm-sure. I love you, you know that. You're my brother, my other half. We're like reflections in Peetre's Pond.'

Noah immediately brightened. 'I like Peetre's Pond,' he said. 'I like it lots. Y'think maybe we can go fishin' there again, just you'n me? One day? Huh?'

'Sure. Don't you know that's the only reason I came back? Just so we could go fuckin' *fishin'* together?'

Stung by Nash's sarcasm, Noah started sobbing again. 'Why you actin' so mean?' he wailed. 'Ain't my fault you keep comin' back. Wh-Why do you, anyway? Huh? Huh?'

Nash eyed him contemptuously. 'Ever hear of an alibi?'

Noah shook his head.

'Means I can't be in two places at once.'

'Why for you wanna be in two places at once?'

'I don't, idiot. That's the whole point.'

'Point? Point of what, huh?'

''Long as I stay around here and pretend like I'm chained up, I can do whatever I want without being punished. Any place else, like Slidell or New Orleans, I do something people don't like, I could go to prison.'

Noah frowned, alarmed. 'You're goin' to prison?'

''Course not, stupid. But if I was in a city and got caught, I might. You understand?'

Noah didn't. But he said anyway: ''Cause you got a point and don't like bein' in two places at once?'

Nash wanted to hit him. But remembering it was useless trying to make his brother understand anything, he grinned and said: 'That's it.'

''Mean I'm right? Huh? Huh?'

'Right as two peas in a pod, *Petit Frère*.'

'Peas?' Noah said, brightening again. 'We gonna shuck peas? I like shuckin' peas.'

'Then go ask Ma if you can shuck

some,' Nash said, tired of dealing with him. 'Go on, *passé!* Bug off and leave me alone.'

Noah pouted and tears ran down his face.

'Aw, sweet Jesus,' Nash said. 'Quit your blubberin', dammit!' He held out his arms to Noah. 'Come here, you big dummy, and I'll give you a hug.'

Noah crossed the chalk line without fear and let his brother embrace him. Nash gently stroked Noah's hair. 'It's okay, Little Brother. Don't cry. I know you can't help it.'

He kissed Noah on the cheek and pushed him toward the door. Noah went reluctantly. From the doorway he looked back, said: 'I love you, Nash. Always will. I'm gonna get some more 'gator teeth for your necklace. You just wait'n see.'

'You make sure you only get teeth that have fallen out natural,' Nash reminded him.

'Sure, sure' Noah said eagerly. 'I can remember that. I know you love 'gators.'

10

At the Slidell Coroner's Office the following morning, Kate looked down at the small, covered corpse of Marie Gaspard on the autopsy table before her and swallowed softly. Les Fields had been right — the Gaspard cabin had indeed been a slaughterhouse.

The bodies of Clovis Gaspard and his wife, Valérie, had been seated across from each other at their old, chrome-legged table as if waiting for a meal they would never eat. In his early thirties, Clovis wore a camo bandana tied around his dark, unruly hair, a white T-shirt now red with blood, and worn blue jeans. He'd been incapacitated by a single stab wound to the lower left back.

His dark, dead eyes had been trading empty stares with those of his wife. In old jeans and a blood-stained yellow tank-top, she had once been attractive in a tall, thin, austere way. Her thick auburn hair had been her best feature. It now hung lankly about her pale face, framing eyes which, before they'd filmed over in death, had been watery-green. Below her small cleft chin her throat had been cut.

The killer had brutally cut off his victims' ears, leaving ugly scab-covered wounds, and then torn out their tongues. Clovis' beard, below his lips, was stiff with caked blood and his wife looked as if she'd buried her lips and chin in strawberry jam.

Both corpses had inch-long numbers carved into their foreheads. Clovis was number 7, his wife number 8.

And the heavily-wrapped, child-sized bundle lying on the table between them — their daughter, Marie — was number 9.

The Butcher had mummified her.

The cabin's walls had been splashed with blood. For the most part the streaks and swirls had appeared to be randomly drawn. But near the window Kate had noticed three distinct shapes — what looked like the handle of an umbrella, a half-circle that could possibly represent a setting sun and another that clearly depicted a leg from the knee down.

Now the county pathologist indicated the child's body and said: 'He didn't remove her ears or tongue, but there was considerable trauma to the face.'

Kate frowned. 'When you say trauma, do you mean he hit her? Cut her up?'

'I mean that he used some kind of hooked instrument to remove most of her brain through her nasal cavity, after which he introduced a mixture of various substances into the resulting space,' the pathologist replied bluntly.

'You saying he tried to *embalm* her?'

Her voice echoed hollowly around the white-tiled room.

'Yes, albeit crudely.'

'But he obviously knew a little about what he was doing?' Rosy said.

'Anyone with a high-school knowledge of chemistry could have done the same thing,' said the pathologist. 'But more than that, he had *ingenuity*. He didn't have the right chemicals for the job, but he had enough know-how to work up a basic facsimile from products he found around the victims' home.'

'Such as?'

'Washing soda, baking powder, salt, anti-freeze, bath salts and what appears to have been illicitly-distilled corn whiskey.'

'Have you been able to identify the knife or instrument he used to remove the brain?' asked Rosy.

'I can tell you it was relatively short, because it didn't quite reach to the top or back of the skull and entirely remove the frontal, parietal and occipital lobes. It was also thick and sturdy — definitely a blade of some kind. It was pierced and had finger grooves, which suggests a folding knife. The hooked end suggests a hunting knife. Does that jibe with what you've already been told?'

'Pretty much. Our people have identified it as a gut-hook knife with a short blade, maybe three-point-five inches, that folds back into the handle.'

'Then it should be reasonably easy to identify,' the pathologist said. 'The blades on knives like that are usually four inches and upwards.'

* * *

Afterward, as they made the short drive back to their temporary base of operations — a basement office in the blocky, nondescript Slidell Police Department building on Sgt Alfred Drive — Kate said: 'Why just her, Rosy? Why not cut off her ears and tongue, like he did the others? It's got to mean something.'

Rosy kept his eyes on the road. 'Perhaps she meant something to him. You know, in his grand scheme of things.'

'Like some kind of religious sacrifice?'

'Works for me.'

'Okay, let's ride that for a moment. But a sacrifice to what, or *whom?*'

'Ahh,' Rosy grinned. 'That's why *you* get the big bucks.'

'Well, run it by Behavioral Analysis, ASAP. Same with those symbols we found. If we're lucky, they may have a precedent. I want personnel checks on all the morgues and funeral homes in St Tammany Parish, too.'

He whistled. 'You don't want much, do you, *jefe?*'

'Our boy's shown some knowledge of

embalming. Can you think of a better place to start?'

'Not at the moment,' Rosy said. 'These mutilations — what's your take on them?'

Kate shrugged. 'I think he cuts off his victims' ears and tongues to silence the voices.'

'What voices?'

'Either the ones he hears in his head or the real ones that boss him around.'

'Like a nagging wife, maybe?'

'Up yours, homey!'

'What'd I say?'

'You think there aren't any nagging *husbands* out there?'

'You know the old saying: 'Men command, women demand.''

'More *barrio* philosophy?'

'Straight from the lips of Pancho Villa.'

Kate laughed, ever thankful for Rosy's irreverent humor. 'God, you are so full of shit.'

He grinned. 'So tell me, Mrs Rathman, whose voices do *you* think he hears?'

'A domineering mother would be my first guess.'

'Okay. No ears, our boy can't hear her

nagging. No tongue, mom has nothing to nag him with. Brilliant.'

'It's only a theory.'

'No, really, I like it. It's a psycho-behavioral profile that not only fits the Bayou Butcher, it also makes me appreciate why Quantico thinks you're a genius.'

'You might change your mind when you hear what else I've come up with.'

He threw her a frown. 'What?'

'A connection,' she murmured thoughtfully. 'With *Egypt*.'

11

Ma Guidry sat alone in a last-row pew in the small shadowy clapboard church, head bowed and hands clasped before her. Her eyes were shut and her fat lips moved urgently in prayer.

Please Dear Lord, help me . . . show me a sign so I can destroy the evil in him . . .

Nash had always been a problem. Even when he was a child there had been something . . . *different* about him. At first Ma had sensed it more than seen it. But eventually it manifested itself in all kinds of ugly ways.

. . . show me a sign so I can destroy the evil in him . . .

At home he was fearless, impulsive and irresponsible. At school he charmed, manipulated and *used*. He was a loner and a compulsive liar, and nothing beyond his own private fantasy world ever held his interest for more than a few moments.

. . . the evil in him . . .

In the fall of 1996, a fishing boat and a cabin cruiser had collided on the Bogue Chitto River. The Coast Guard retrieved four bodies, but the fifth was never found. Two weeks later Noah came running out of the woods, hollering for his mother. Ma could still see his eight year-old face streaked with tears, his chest heaving so violently he couldn't speak.

Stammering, he explained that the missing corpse had washed up on a shoal in Middle Creek. He and Nash had found it by accident. Nash wanted to keep it a secret, but Noah was so frightened by the corpse, he ran home.

Eventually Ma coaxed him into taking her to the body. Reluctantly he led her through the swamp to a bank overhung with Spanish moss. Here, she found Nash crouched over the corpse. Once a large man of about thirty, the body was now so bloated and disfigured by fish bites, Ma barely recognized it as a human being.

What was even more repulsive was the sight of her eldest son, Nash, fondling the corpse's ears and muttering to it as if it were a plaything.

Sickened, Ma had screamed at him and tried to drag him away. Instantly he turned on her, threatening her with his fists, his mismatched blue-gray eyes flashing with anger. She'd glared at him, seeing in her mind a young version of her mean-spirited ex-husband, Peyton.

'I'm warnin' you, boy,' she said finally. 'Get away from there or I'll beat you bloody.'

'The hell you will!' Nash said. 'Leave me alone!' And then, chillingly: 'Leave *us* alone!'

Ma angrily cuffed him about the head. Nash stumbled back, stunned. Before he could recover, she grabbed him and dragged him home. He'd cursed her every step of the way.

That incident confirmed what Ma had always chosen to ignore: there was something horribly *wrong* with Nash. But instead of sending him to a therapist she couldn't possibly afford, she decided to trust in God and hope that her son would eventually grow out of whatever sickness ailed him.

He never did.

Late one afternoon a few months later she caught Nash torturing a baby raccoon in the woodshed. Later, digging in some suspiciously fresh dirt behind the shed, she found the grisly remains of a squirrel, a bat snake and a young buck — all brutally disfigured by a knife.

Still she prayed for God to save him. And for a while, as he grew older, he did seem to change for the better. But in hindsight she realized that he had only been biding his time.

The Bible — *John 8:44* — had been right all along. *You are of your father the devil, and your will is to do your father's desires. He was a murderer from the beginning, and has nothing to do with the truth —*

And a voice inside her, a voice she would later convince herself was God's, told her she must stop him from ever inflicting his own particular brand of evil on the world. If he should ever leave home, no one would be safe. And Ma couldn't live with that. Not and still live with God.

So she had made her decision and that same night had acted upon it. She'd laced his supper with compounded laudanum. Old Olivie Melancon, who knew about such things, had mixed it for her several months ago, when Ma had suffered an attack of *le fritch*. The laudanum had stopped the diarrhea, but it had also knocked her out. Ma hoped it would do the same to Nash. It should, because Olivie had promised her that the potion grew more potent with age.

It worked. Nash fell asleep right after supper and when he woke up next morning, he found himself chained to the iron frame of his bed, a prisoner. The barred window and the hardened steel Trojan ground anchor had come later.

Nash had ranted for days. Luckily, their neighbors were too far off to hear him, and Ma had ordered Noah to stay away from his brother. Grudgingly, he obeyed. But all that week he'd constantly wanted to know how long she intended to keep Nash chained up.

'Till the devil's starved out of him,' she said.

'How long'll that be? Huh? Huh?'

'Till God gives me a sign, boy. Now quit your yappin' an' get back to your chores.'

But God had never given her a sign. And now, four years later, she knew she could wait no longer. She was dying. Her body was shutting down on her and there wasn't a single thing she could do to stop it. The slightest exertion left her breathless and clutching at her chest, the pain there so acute she almost blacked out. Then all she could do was sit on the couch, perfectly still, her immense body covered in sweat, arms two dead weights, pulse hammering, and wait for the pain to subside.

So far she'd survived. But she knew it was only a matter of time. Eventually her heart would give out. And then what would happen to her boys? Noah relied on her for almost everything. No one else would look after him the way she had.

As for Nash . . . who would look after *him?* Who would keep him chained up?

Certainly not Noah. Nash would persuade his brother to unchain him even before her blood cooled. After that he would be free to torture and murder at will . . .

Ma's sob of despair echoed inside the empty church.

Too weary to pray any more, she struggled to her feet. Crossing herself before the altar, she left the old lavender-smelling church and started home.

It was late afternoon. Moss-green shadows dappled the thin winding path that Ma followed through the trees. She'd only gone a short distance when she sensed she was being followed. She stopped and looked back. The path was empty and she blamed her uneasiness on her imagination.

She lumbered on, wheezing in the damp, suffocating heat. Presently she heard the snap of a branch behind her. She looked back. Dusk had fallen without her realizing. On either side of the path the dense swamp had grown still and silent.

'Anyone there?' she hollered.

Silence. But she wasn't fooled. She could sense a presence.

'Who is it?' she called. 'Whyn't you show yo'self?'

A shadowy figure melted out of the trees and stood, motionless before her.

Her breath caught in her throat.

It was her husband, Peyton.

He'd changed almost beyond recognition in the last fifteen years. Gone was the muscular, handsome man whose dark hair, devilish blue eyes and wild, unruly ways had once captivated her. In his place stood a thin, bowed, haggard-faced ex-con who exuded an air of defeat. He wore a long, ill-fitting Confederate-gray overcoat over a wrinkled white shirt and blue jeans, and laced-up black boots.

He came closer, his former swagger now replaced by a weary shuffle. His once-broad shoulders now sagged. The hands he always carried in fists now hung loose, the fingers long and twitchy.

'Bekah?' he said. He made it sound like a question because she too had changed and was no longer recognizable as the voluptuous, curvy girl he'd made pregnant at a local picnic and then been forced to marry.

It had been years since anyone had called her by her given name. And though he'd said it gently, she wasn't fooled. Peyton Guidry had always been a Godless man given to strange, heathen beliefs, a violent, abusive, self-centered man who shunned work and took what he wanted by force — including her. Oh, he might have changed physically, but inside she was sure he was still the same black soul.

'I heard you got out,' she said uneasily. 'But I never thought you'd have the nerve to show up 'round here again.'

'Why not? This is the only home I got.'

'You got no home here.'

'Not with you, maybe. You made that clear enough. Not once in fifteen years did you come visit me.'

'Then we both know where we stand, don't we?'

'How're the boys?' he asked.

'They's fine. Just fine.'

'Still livin' at home?'

'*Oui.*'

'Thought Nash might've married by now and given me some *petits enfants*.' When she didn't answer, he said: 'I want to see them.'

Ma snorted. 'You ain't been in their lives since they was eight years old, an' you got no place in their lives now.'

'That's for them to say. They're of an age.'

Ma knew she couldn't let that happen. Peyton had loved both boys, but Nash was always his favorite. If he ever found out that Nash was chained up, he'd kill her and set him free, never knowing the evil he was committing.

'It'd just be a waste of time. Far as they's concerned, you're good as dead. They don't even remember you now.'

'I don't believe that,' Peyton said.

'Believe what you want. Don't change nothin'. Moment you robbed that gas station, they was done with you. So was I. Don't think you can buy your way back into our lives again now.'

'I'll hear that from them,' he insisted.

'What you'll hear if'n you come sniffin' around, is my pistol goin' off in your face.

I'll kill you, Peyton. Before God, I swear it. Them boys has had a hard life 'cause of you and your wicked ways. You try to see them and I swear to Almighty Jehovah, I'll kill you.'

He looked into her puffy, angry eyes and knew she meant it. He didn't want to back down, but he was on probation and any trouble would land him back in prison. Swallowing his anger, he said: 'All right, Bekah, you made your point. But one way or another I *will* see my boys. I got rights too, you know.'

Turning, he melted back into the trees.

Her last memory of him was seeing his heavy Confederate coat flapping around his calves.

12

Kate knew Rosy wasn't completely sold on her theory yet, and waited until they were in their basement office, standing before the rows of 8 x 10 photographs that were pinned to a cork-board, before trying to convince him. The photos showed the Butcher's victims in chronological order: the Rivets seated at a picnic table, all dead, their ears and tongues removed; the Clemenceaus gathered about a dinner table, all similarly mutilated; and the Gaspards, with little Marie as the main course.

'Think about it, homey,' she said. 'We have an alligator tooth, an attempt at embalming and a crude stab — if you'll forgive the pun — at mummification. What does that say to you?'

'That our boy's one sick fuck.'

'Agreed. But if you're not ready to buy Egypt yet, answer me this: How's the brain usually removed prior to embalming?'

Rosy thought a moment. 'The embalmer

makes a saw-cut in the back of the head, doesn't he?'

'Correct. But in ancient Egypt the brain was removed *through the nasal cavity, using a hook.*'

'The way it was with Marie.'

'*Exactly* the way it was with Marie. Then there's that concoction our boy cooked up to embalm her. It's similar to natron.'

'Which is . . . ?'

'The Egyptian equivalent to modern-day embalming fluid. It was a mixture of sodium carbonate and sodium bicarbonate, intended to dry out the body.'

'Which is why he used soda, baking powder and salt from the Gaspard kitchen.'

'Could be.'

'There's just one flaw in your theory, boss: there are no alligators in Egypt. Just crocodiles.'

She said, as if he hadn't spoken: 'There's one other thing we should consider. Remember those drawings at the Gaspard place?'

'The severed leg and all that other stuff?'

'What if they weren't just drawings? What if they were hieroglyphics?'

'O-kaay,' he said.

'You still don't buy it.'

'Let's just say I'm exhibiting a healthy scepticism.'

'All right. Let's check it out, if only to discount it.'

He opened his laptop and booted it up. Kate stood over him. 'Try 'Mummification and Embalming',' she said.

He tapped in the term and hit *Search*. It returned more than 50,000 results. Every one of them on the first page linked the processes to Egypt.

'Now try 'Alligators'.'

He did so. The term brought in almost two million results, but nothing immediately linking the term to Egypt.

Undaunted, she said: 'Type in 'Hieroglyphs.'' Then: 'No, it's *i* before *e*.'

'Gotcha.'

The top result out of more than 700,000 was *Hieroglyphics Ancient Egyptian Writing and Alphabet Translator*. But there were a number of charts above the result and Rosy clicked on the largest.

'Let's see what we've got.'

'There's our leg,' she pointed. 'It translates as *B*.'

'Coincidence?'

'No. Look,' she pointed again. 'What do you see there?'

He saw a bowl with a small handle. 'The image we thought was either the setting sun or a half-circle?'

'And it translates as a *K*.'

He checked the chart again. 'But there's nothing that looks like the handle of an umbrella.'

'Go back and try another chart.'

He did so. The next chart that came up was too detailed to make any sense. But the one after that was simplified, a straightforward alphabet based on Egyptian symbols.

'There,' she pointed. 'It's an *S*, Rosy.'

'If you say so, boss.'

'What do you mean? It's there in black and white.'

'So's the description. And *it* claims that squiggle's supposed to be a bolt of cloth. Doesn't look like a bolt of cloth to me.'

'Don't be so negative. We've got

111

something here, *hombre.* I know we have. *B, K, S.*'

'The killer's initials?'

'Or maybe an abbreviation?'

'Short for Books, you mean?'

'Could be.'

'How about 'Barracks.''

'Our boy's military?'

'That's if we've got the letters in the right sequence.'

Kate turned to the board and studied the photographs of the cabin walls. 'Working from left to right we get *S B K.*'

He typed in *SBK Acronyms* and studied what came up. 'Hmmm. What do you make of this?'

'Single Below Knee,' she read. 'Fits with the Egyptian symbol for *B.*'

'And possibly an amputation fantasy.'

'What else you got?'

'Small Business Knowledge, Standard Boat Kit . . . '

'That works. Our boy travels through the swamp by boat. He has to.'

'Sensor Bracket Kit . . . Skippy Bush Kangaroo . . . '

She giggled. 'Shit, I must be getting

tired. I thought that was funny.'

'I am a very funny man, *senorita*,' Rosy deadpanned.

'You're getting tired too,' Kate said. Then, all business: 'All right, let's refine our search. Try . . . 'SBK Egypt'.'

His fingers tapped the keys and then *Search*.

Nothing.

'Try 'SBK Embalming.''

He did.

She whispered: 'Oh, Christ.'

He was looking at it, too.

Anubis Ancient Egyptian God
Sobek **(sbk)** — Thoth Egyptian God thumbnail . . . Anubis is considered to have invented **embalming**

'Try 'SBK mummification',' she said. He did.

The number one result read:

Anubis, Ancient Egyptian God
Sobek (sbk) — Thoth Egyptian God thumbnail. Thoth . . . Anubis invented mummification to preserve human

bodies, and presided over the funeral rituals . . .

'Good enough,' she said. 'Now let's see what we've got for this Sobek.'

He typed in *sobek*.

A series of illustrations came on screen, depicting a dark-skinned Egyptian in ancient style, holding an *ankh* — the Egyptian symbol for eternal life — in his right hand. Though he had the body of a man, his head was that of a crocodile.

Below it, the first search result read:

Sobek
Sobek (also known as Sebek, Sebek-Ra, Sobeq, Suchos, Sobki, and Soknopais) was the ancient god of crocodiles. He is first mentioned in the Pyramid Texts and . . .

'*Ea diache!*' Rosy murmured. 'I think we're onto somethin' here, boss.'

'Me too, homey,' she replied. 'But *what*, exactly?'

13

That afternoon, when Elliott Ward came out of his hotel bedroom at the Atlanta Ritz-Carlton, he found Chelsea sprawled on the couch, talking on her cell phone and watching re-runs of *The Hills* on TV. He signaled that he wanted to talk to her, but she ignored him. Irked, he grabbed the remote, turned off the TV and stood in front of her.

Chelsea said, 'Hang on,' into the phone, and then glared at her father. 'I was watching that,' she said indignantly.

'After I leave you can watch it again,' Elliott said. 'Now, how do I look?'

Resigned, she gave him a quick once-over. 'You're supposed to wear a blue shirt, remember?'

'I don't have one. So I put on a blue tie instead.'

She rolled her big, apple-green eyes. 'Dad, you are so *dumb!* They asked you to wear a blue shirt because it comes across better on TV.'

'Oh.' Quickly, because she was already reaching for the remote, he added: 'You think maybe I should stop and get one on the way?'

'Whatever.'

About to continue her telephone conversation, she saw that he was still watching her, waiting for something more. 'What?' she asked.

'I was, uh, just wondering.'

''Bout what?'

'Kate. What you thought of her?'

Chelsea shrugged. 'She was okay.'

'That good, huh?'

'Well, what do you want me to say?'

'Nothing, I guess,' he said, hiding his disappointment.

'Now, what?' she said as he still stood there.

'Remember, you're not to leave this room under any circumstances.'

'Already said I wouldn't.'

'Just wanted to make sure we're on the same page.'

'Anything else?'

He wanted to tell her that a little

politeness wouldn't hurt, but he knew it would only cause an argument. So instead he pecked her on the cheek. "Bye, sweetheart. Watch the show,' and left.

Before the door even closed Chelsea had turned the TV back on and put the phone to her ear. 'Sorry. Dad was freaking out again. What? Yeah, he's gonna be on *Larry Kent Live* tonight . . . to promote his book, I guess . . . I could have, yeah, but I didn't want to . . . 'Cause I didn't, that's why. Now will you please shut up about my dad so I can finish telling you what Brad said . . . '

14

Up in his room, Nash was thinking about the experiment he'd conducted on Marie.

The ancient Egyptians had believed that preservation of the mummy empowered the soul after death, which would return to the preserved corpse. His books — *Pa's* books — were filled with such references. Nash doubted very much that Marie would ever come back, but there was always that chance. It would be fascinating if she did.

Thinking of his beloved books inevitably made Nash think of Pa, whom he'd idolized. It also reminded him of the constant fighting between his parents. As far back as he could remember they had always argued, usually over Pa's lazy ways, his drinking and their constant lack of money, and Ma's obsession with God and the Holy Bible. Their quarrels always seemed to start at mealtimes, soon escalating into screaming matches that often chased Nash and Noah crying from the table.

But despite their dislike for one another, both parents always found time for their boys. Pa especially was always there for them. He took them hunting and fishing, and to Peetre's Pond where together they built the tree-house. Later, he'd shown them how to build a small pirogue and maneuver the flat-bottomed boat through the dense swamp. And on nights when it was too hot for sleep he'd come up to their room, sit on the edge of the bed and tell them stories until they finally drifted off.

Nash's favorite story was about Pa and the alligator. As a boy, Pa had been walking alone in the bayous, when a 'gator exploded out of the murky water and attacked him.

Pa leapt back, barely avoiding its jaws, and tried to run. But trees blocked his escape. The 'gator pursued him, stopping only when it was a few feet away. Pa froze, jelly-legged and terrified, waiting for it to attack.

It never did. The huge scaly reptile

studied him with cold, dead eyes . . . and then slowly turned and slipped back into the water.

Pa stood there, trembling, trying to figure out why the 'gator hadn't dragged him away.

He never did find the answer; not in his mind or in the public library in Slidell. But in the process of reading every book, magazine and article he could find on 'gators and crocodiles, he'd become fascinated with the reptiles. Slowly, as money afforded, he'd assembled a collection of books about them and about ancient Egyptian history, with which they were so closely linked.

After hearing the story, Nash also wondered why the 'gator let his father live. He agreed with Pa, who always felt it had to be more than just luck. 'Way I see it, son, Fate was savin' me for some important purpose.'

Now, as Nash gazed at the books on the shelf, he wondered what that purpose was. God had never given Pa anything important to do or even sent him a sign. Instead, the day after the twins' eighth birthday, he'd been arrested for armed robbery. 'Your Pa's gone to prison,' Ma had told them when they came home from school, 'and he ain't never comin' back.'

Noah was upset and bawled; Nash was shattered. Over time he became increasingly angry and withdrawn. He also found increased pleasure in torturing and killing small animals. But even their pain couldn't take away the agony of losing his father. Nothing could.

Then came the day when Ma chained him up. And when it became obvious even to him that there would be no escape, he'd sought solace in Pa's books. He'd read them over and over, each time growing more fascinated with 'gators. Like Pa, he was especially captivated by Sobek, the ancient Egyptian crocodile god, to whom those who worked along the Nile prayed for protection against crocodile attack.

Sobek was seen by his followers as the embodiment of strength and power, traits Nash had always admired. But his admiration turned to obsession when he discovered that Sobek was also revered as a 'repairer of evil.' The same night he dreamed that Sobek spoke to him, promising to return his father to him — if Nash was brave enough to pay the price.

'To redeem a loved one,' Sobek had told him, 'three by three by three must pay.'

When Nash awoke the next morning, the dream was still fresh in his mind. He took it to be a sign and knew that he must follow Sobek's instructions. He'd already read about how three and multiples of three were sacred numbers in Egyptian mythology, so it wasn't hard to figure out that Sobek demanded 27 sacrifices before he would bring Pa back. As far as Nash was concerned, it was a small price to pay.

For four years he hadn't been able to do anything but fantasize about his quest. Then Noah had found Ma's spare key to his padlock and . . . Nash was free to fulfill his task.

It had not occurred to him then that he too could become a repairer of evil; but after he'd claimed his first three sacrifices, the Clemenceaus, he'd heard their shrill voices arguing in his head. They'd reminded him of his own unhappy home life. He looked at the bodies, at the picnic table outside and realized that God had given him a chance to make everything right. Thrilled, he cut out the Clemenceaus' tongues so they could never shout at anyone again, and sliced off their ears so they would never have to listen to anyone arguing the way he and Noah had, and in a final flash of inspiration had dragged the bodies out to the picnic table and posed them as a perfect family group.

Peace at mealtime.

It was wonderful.

15

Under the glaring lights of CNN's Studio B, Larry Kent held up a copy of *Surgical Secrets of the Psychopathic Mind* and said to his guest: 'I have to tell you, Elliott, I found this absolutely fascinating — and easy to understand, too.'

Elliott, immaculate in a new blue shirt and contrasting tie, smiled appreciatively from the other side of his host's trademark desk. 'I'm glad to hear that, because I deliberately tried to avoid surgeon-speak so the layman could grasp the procedure.'

'Worked for me,' said Kent. 'And the subject really seems to have gotten people fired up. But before we go to the phones, let's just clarify this a little. You've already told us what Deep Brain Stimulation *is*, but how exactly does it *work*?'

'Good question. I only wish I had a good answer. But I don't. As I told my daughter Chelsea, who's out of school and traveling with me on this tour, the truth is that we still don't really know for sure *why* it works, only that it *does*.'

'So what's your own personal take on it?'

Elliott picked up the glass of water at his elbow and thought for a moment. Before him, the studio audience fell expectantly quiet.

'Picture this,' he said at last. 'I'm sitting here being interviewed by you, and even though the mood in the studio is friendly enough, I'm irritated by something you said and suddenly I think: 'I've had it with this guy. I'm going to prove to the audience that he doesn't intimidate me.' So right here, on live TV, I pick up my glass, intending to dump water all over you.'

Kent faked a look of horror. 'Uh-oh! You think I should *leave* now?'

Elliott joined in the audience's laughter. 'No,' he said. 'You're safe. Because, even though in that moment it's what I want to do, I don't do it. Instead, I just take a sip of water, like this — ' he did so

' — and then I put my glass down and no one's any the wiser as to just how close I came to making tomorrow's headlines. But why *didn't* I pour that water over your head?'

'Tell me.'

'The answer lies here, in my brain. An impulse there suggested what I was going to do, but before I could act upon it, an *inhibitory reaction* kicked in and stopped me. And that's what happens to most of us every minute of every day.

'In essence, these inhibitory brain cells keep us in line. But in some individuals, those cells don't always function, so there's nothing to make them stop and consider the consequences of whatever they propose to do. That's where DBS comes into it. By sending electrical pulses to certain regions of the brain, we can activate, *de*activate or interrupt specific impulses.'

'And by the same process,' said Kent, 'you're saying that DBS can be used on serial killers and other social misfits to effectively give them the conscience they otherwise don't have.'

'Exactly,' said Elliott. 'Once the neuro-transmitters are implanted, the electrical stimulation required to activate, deactivate or interrupt specific parts or paths in the brain can be non-invasively adjusted to meet each patient's individual need.'

'Amazing.'

'Sure. And though this procedure is still at the experimental stage, I'm hopeful that one day soon it will successfully turn dangerous psychopaths into normal, sociable human beings.'

Clearly impressed, the host turned to the camera and said: 'Don't go away, folks. We'll be back to take your calls right after these messages.'

⋆   ⋆   ⋆

In her cramped, darkened living room, Ma stared at Elliott's image on the TV screen and muttered: 'Hallelujah . . . '

Noah was sitting cross-legged beside her, feeding lettuce to his pet turtle, Pookie. He looked up in surprise as Ma reached for a handkerchief and blotted the tears streaming down her fat cheeks.

'What's wrong, Ma? What is it? What? You okay? Huh?'

Ignoring him, Ma clasped her hands tight, closed her eyes and whispered fervently: 'Thank you, Oh Lord, for answerin' my prayers . . . '

16

The support team Kate requested late that afternoon arrived early the following morning. Special Agent Jason Hicks was a muscular black man in his early thirties with gold-rimmed glasses, and Special Agent Jane Fuller a bright, articulate, quietly confident young woman who had turned down a Rhode's Scholarship to Oxford to join the FBI.

They joined Kate and Rosy in their temporary basement office where Kate introduced them to Deputy Doucet. There because he was the liaison between the Bureau and the St Tammany Parish Sheriff's Office, he was tight-mouthed as usual and sat at the back of the room, alone.

Kate wasted no time in bringing the agents up to speed. 'We've established a tentative but definite link between the Butcher and ancient Egypt, but we're not sure how it figures in this thing just yet.

That's where you guys come in.'

'What's the link?' asked Fuller.

'The hieroglyphs we found on the walls of the Gaspard shack spell 'SBK' or *Sobek*. Sobek was the ancient god of crocodiles.'

Deputy Doucet cleared his throat impatiently. 'Are you *serious* about this?'

'You don't buy it?'

'Let's just say I'm more interested in things we *can* follow up.'

'Forensics, you mean?'

'Beats speculation, wouldn't you say?'

Rosy saw Kate's jaw clench and quickly said: 'We know some things for sure. We know he's young and fit, we know he's local, that he's left-handed, that he wears size ten boots, and that he's never been in trouble before, otherwise his prints would be on file. Overnight the lab has also been able to isolate the various components used in the production of the gloves he wears, and narrowed them down to two brands, Usave and Gripp.'

Kate's phone buzzed. She looked at the caller ID, then slipped it back in her pocket and faced Doucet. 'The fact remains, Deputy, this is a significant discovery and we're going to run with it.'

'You're the boss,' Deputy Doucet said.

Ignoring him, Kate turned to Agents Hicks and Fuller: 'It's also significant that our boy kills in groups of three. The number is important in Egyptian beliefs. So are its multiples.'

'Meaning?' asked Agent Hicks.

'If he's multiplied three by three, then he's killed the nine people he set out to kill, and if we don't catch him soon he stands an excellent chance of getting away with it.'

'But you don't believe that,' said Hicks.

'I don't. Killing's an addiction with these sickos. They don't give it up so easily.'

'So you're saying . . . ?'

'He's aiming for the next multiple up — three times three times three. Twenty-seven.'

Agent Fuller paled. 'Jesus.'

Deputy Doucet had heard enough. 'If you people don't mind, I got things to do . . . '

'I'm sure you do,' Kate said.

Agent Fuller waited until the Deputy had left, then said: 'So what's our next step?'

'If there's any kind of crocodile-worshipping cult out there, no matter how small or obscure, I want to know about it before the end of the day.'

'I'm on it,' said Fuller.

'Hicks, find yourself a desk and a phone. I want you to call all the museums and zoos within a twenty-mile radius. Get them to check the personnel records of everyone who's worked for them in the last two years. No, make it three, just to be sure. What we're looking for is anyone who has a particular interest in or an affinity with crocs and alligators that might be considered unusual or suspicious. Same with the zoos. Maybe someone's noticed a regular visitor who spends most of his time hanging around the alligator exhibits.'

'What about me?' Rosy asked.

'I want you to find us a psychologist who specializes in mind control. I'd like to know what kind of person would be most likely to join such a cult.'

'And where will you be if I need to reach you?'

She thought about the call she'd just received from Elliott. 'I want to study up some more on Sobek.'

'Good idea,' Rosy said. ''Cause if we've got this wrong, boss, Deputy Dawg's never gonna let us live it down.'

17

The desk clerk at the Ritz-Carlton checked the register before saying to his caller: 'No, ma'am, Dr Ward is no longer lecturing here . . . I believe New Orleans . . . Yes, yes. The Plaza. Yes, ma'am. You're welcome.'

★　★　★

Ma Guidry hung up.

For a moment she stood beside the payphone at the back of Jean Leblanc's dingy general store, thinking. All around her were shelves filled with *Slap Ya Mama* spices and barrels overflowing with weighed bags of beans, oats and grains.

As she fished in her purse for more coins, she glanced over one shoulder. Behind his counter by the door, Leblanc was crouched over a bench-vise, trying to teach Noah how to make a lure.

She set down her change and took out

a creased scrap of paper and a pencil-stub. When she was ready, she picked up the phone, dialed 411 and said: 'I want the number of the Plaza Hotel, in New Orleans.'

★ ★ ★

The bellhop opened the door to the elegant 6th floor suite and said: 'Welcome to the Big Easy, Dr Ward.'

Elliott thanked him. 'We've been looking forward to our stay, haven't we, Chels'?'

Chelsea gave a shrug that could have meant anything.

The bellhop drew back the blinds, revealing the sprawl of New Orleans below them. Elliott tipped him, waited until he'd left and then joined Chelsea at the window. The skyline was a panorama of blocky, modern skyscrapers all standing watch over the Mississippi and the ships that plied her waters.

'Just think, Chels'. Jazz was born out there.'

When she didn't reply, he said: 'Look, sweetheart, I know this hasn't been much fun for you, and for that I'm sorry. But

135

this is our last stop, so what do you say we put everything behind us and just have a great time, okay?'

'I'll try,' she said.

He pecked her on the forehead. 'Listen. I have some calls to make, but after that I'm all yours. How about we go out and grab a bite? See some sights while we're at it?'

'Whatever.'

Elliott gave up. Entering his bedroom, he picked up the phone and called Kate. He got her voice-mail. He paused, not sure what to say, then left a message saying that he and Chelsea had just arrived, were staying at The Plaza, and would she please call him.

As he hung up, Chelsea appeared in the doorway. 'Hey, Dad. Want me to unpack your stuff, like mom used to?'

It was the last thing he wanted. Shannon had always been meticulous about their clothes. Everything was neatly folded or hung exactly where it should be. Chelsea, by contrast, was a pull-off-and-throw-in-the-corner kind of girl. But not wanting to upset her, he said: 'Great idea, sweetheart.'

Beside him, the phone rang. He snatched it up, thinking it might be Kate returning his call. 'Hello?'

There was no immediate reply, only the sound of someone breathing. Then a voice said: 'Dr Ward?'

Elliott frowned. 'Yes. Who is this?'

'I saw you on TV last night,' said Ma, keeping her voice low.

'I'm sorry, you'll have to speak up.'

She raised her voice a little. 'That *opération* you was talkin' about. I think maybe it could make my son better.'

Elliott said: 'How did you get this number?'

Ignoring him, she went on: 'I mean, he's not sick or nothin', but he's ill, in the mind. This *opération*, it would cure him, *oui?*'

'Listen, ma'am, if your son has a problem, he should see his own physician.'

'He ain't got no physician. All he's got is me — an' maybe you, if you'll operate on him.'

Elliott said as diplomatically as he could: 'I'm sorry, ma'am, it doesn't work that way.'

137

'Then how *does* it work?'

'Ma'am — '

'*Please,*' she said. 'I got to know.'

He sighed. 'Well, for a start, the patient has to fit certain criteria. He has to undergo a psychological evaluation to show that he would benefit from the surgery, and then of course we have to make sure he's fit enough to undergo the procedure. But most importantly, he'd have to undergo it willingly.'

'But the surgery . . . it would kill the evil in him, *oui?*'

'That's one way of putting it, I guess. It would certainly moderate psychopathic behavior, I'm sure of that. But we're still a long way from performing this procedure on a human patient.'

'You won't help me then?' Ma said. 'Even though my boy needs *le sirugie* to kill the demons in him?'

'I'm sorry, ma'am — '

'You *got* to help! You the only chance he's got!'

'Listen, lady, if your son's ill, you need to get him to a psychiatrist to be evaluated. Okay?'

'But *you* can fix him.'

'Ma'am,' Elliott said firmly, 'please don't call this number again.'

He hung up.

★ ★ ★

The line went dead in Ma's ear. She wiped angry tears away, wondering why God had shown her a way to cure Nash, only to then steal it from her again.

Twisting her handkerchief, she wished she'd never seen the show. Then she never would've built her hopes up. She told herself there must be some other way to cure the evil in Nash, but what was it? The closest she'd ever come was this operation. It was torture to think that Dr Ward could make things right for Nash, and yet chose not to.

She considered calling him again, trying to appeal to him as a mother . . . After all, he too was a parent. What would he do if his *daughter* was stricken with the same evil?

But even as she considered it, she knew it would do no good. This *docteur*, he was more interested in selling his book and making money than helping her. There was nothing to be gained from that, no fame or fortune.

Unless . . .

Unless she could somehow *force* him to help her.

A dark thought stirred inside her.

The idea of kidnapping a child would have normally made her drop to her knees and pray for deliverance. But maybe that thought, as evil as it was, was in some way justified. After all, she'd tried to do the right thing by asking Dr Ward for help. It wasn't her fault that he had refused her.

In those circumstances perhaps her idea wasn't as dark as it first appeared. Perhaps it was simply a means to an end, a way to get the doctor to reconsider and perform *l'opération* after all. A bargain, if you liked.

Cure my boy, and I spare your girl.

★ ★ ★

Once they'd finished unpacking, Elliott and Chelsea set out to explore the city.

The French Quarter wasn't like anything Chelsea had ever seen before, full of narrow, tourist-filled streets, ornate horse-drawn carriages and brightly colored buildings with filigreed wrought-iron balconies.

At the Riverwalk Marketplace Elliott bought her an abstract-print sundress, a cropped tee-shirt she just *had* to have and two ridiculously expensive Daisy de Villeneuve candles.

As they were leaving the mall she spotted a plaited leather friendship bracelet. She didn't ask him to buy it. But Elliott, by now caught up in the fun of shopping, insisted she have it and paid extra to have her initials burned into it.

Finally, exhausted and hungry, they stopped for *beignets* at the Café du Monde, on Decatur Street. As they were enjoying the sugared pastries, Elliott's cell phone buzzed. He checked the caller ID. His face lit up as he saw it was Kate.

'Hi,' he said. 'So you got my message?'

'Yep. Are you guys having a fun time?'

'Wonderful.' He glanced at Chelsea who was busy texting someone. ''Least, I hope so.'

'That's great,' Kate said. 'Look, Elliott, about dinner. I'm sorry but I have to pass.'

'Oh.'

'I'd love to — really. But we're jammed here.' Out the corner of her eye she saw Rosy shoot her a questioning look and then continue studying the crime scene photos pinned on the corkboard. 'But I'd love a rain-check.'

'Sure,' Elliott said hollowly. 'If you can't, you can't.'

There was an awkward pause as neither knew what to say next. Kate again looked at Rosy, who was now thumbing through the phone book. He gave her a look of mock disbelief and mouthed: *Is someone actually asking you out on a date?*

She gave him the finger. He grinned and made a kissy face.

Elliott said: 'Are you sure you won't change your mind?'

'Yes, I, uh . . . Elliott, hang on a sec',' Kate said as Rosy approached. Then covering the mouthpiece: 'What?'

'Confucius say: All work and no play make Jill a dull girl.'

Kate rolled her eyes. 'Butt out, homey. This is a *personal* conversation. *Entendido?*'

'No such thing as *personal* between you and me, *querida.*'

He was right. After all they'd gone through together they might as well have been joined at the hip — which was perhaps why she felt slightly embarrassed discussing a potential date in front of him.

'If you got the chance to go out for the evening,' Rosy added, 'jump at it. I can keep an eye on things here.'

'But what if something breaks?'

'I'll call you.'

'But he's in New Orleans.'

'So what? Go book yourself into a hotel, stay over and have *fun.* You *do* remember what that is, don't you?'

'Up yours,' Kate said. Then as Rosy grinned and returned to his desk, she said into the phone: 'That was my personal advisor. Says I should go out and enjoy myself.'

'Terrific. What time?'

'Oh I dunno. Sevenish, okay?'

'Perfect,' Elliott said. 'We'll meet you in the lobby.'

Elliott hung up and turned to Chelsea. 'That was Kate. She's joining us for dinner.'

'Thanks for telling me.'

Sensing that the bridges they'd built throughout the day were about to collapse, he said: 'I'm sorry. You're right. I should've checked with you first. Is it okay?'

'Does it matter?'

'It matters to *me*.'

They went on eating in silence. Then, out of left field, Chelsea said: 'You really like her, don't you?'

'Kate? Honey, I've known her since college.'

'But you married mom.'

'Of course I did. That was the difference between them. I liked Kate, but I *loved* your mother.'

Chelsea nodded and idly checked her text messages.

Knowing she was shutting him out, he said: 'You still think I'm responsible for Mom's death, don't you?'

144

'Well, it was your idea that she go to that fundraiser.'

'Actually, it was your mother's. She knew I was tied up at the hospital and offered to take my place. But I did agree to it, so you're right — I *am* responsible. But only for her going, not for two taxis colliding on a rainy night.'

Chelsea didn't look up from her cell, so he couldn't tell what she was thinking. 'The funny thing is,' he added bitterly, 'you don't have to blame me for what happened. I'm doing a great job of that all by myself.'

Her mother's death had torn her apart, and afterward she'd been terrified that her father might be next. What would she do then? The thought of being alone made her feel frighteningly vulnerable. In emotional turmoil, she made a snap decision. After that she deliberately distanced herself from her Dad, not because she wanted to hurt him but because she wanted to spare herself the agony of losing someone she loved so much ever again.

Now, as she saw how unhappy he was,

she said suddenly: 'I like her.'

Elliott came back from far-off. 'W-What?'

'Kate — I like her. She's cool.'

'Yeah,' he said, smiling. 'She is, isn't she?'

'Know what?'

'What, sweetheart?'

'She kind of reminds me of Mom.'

18

It was early afternoon when Ma left the wetlands and tree-lined service road that led to Honey Island Swamp and turned onto Gause Boulevard. Her old VW camper, rust showing through its chipped blue paint, lurched and spewed smoke each time she changed gears, and Ma prayed that the engine wouldn't give out before she reached New Orleans. It was only about fifty miles, roundtrip, but as she'd often seen on TV, traffic could bog down on the bridge across Lake Pontchartrain and she was afraid that if they were stuck there too long the engine might overheat or perhaps die altogether, and then she and Noah wouldn't be able to get to the city. And she *had* to get there. Nash's future depended upon it.

Beside her, Noah hummed tunelessly as he rocked back and forth in his seat, nose pressed against the window, eyes riveted on the passing scenery. He'd never been outside of Honey Island before, and wouldn't be leaving it now except that Ma knew she needed his help to accomplish her goal.

Of course, asking her slow-witted son to help her, or do anything for that matter, could turn into a liability. His attention span was almost non-existent and his memory not much better. But she had no other choice. And with God's help . . .

Ma went over her plan again. Now that she knew Dr Ward was at the Plaza in New Orleans, she only needed to choose the right moment to kidnap his daughter. It should be away from the hotel, somewhere quiet, without witnesses — an alley or empty building, maybe. There she would threaten the doctor with Peyton's old .45, forcing him to keep still while Noah dragged his daughter off to the camper. Ma would then tell Dr Ward that the only way he'd get his daughter back, unharmed, was to agree to cure Nash by operating on him.

Later, of course, there'd be consequences. She was under no delusions there. The law wouldn't let her get away with kidnapping. But what could they do to her boys? She'd swear they were innocent; that this was all her idea. Then the law would have no choice but to let them go. And as for her . . . well, she had nothing to lose. She was dying anyway. In fact, she'd probably be dead long before the case ever came to trial.

She drove on. Ahead, bathed in afternoon sunlight, she could see the skyline of New Orleans. It was beautiful, all the tall buildings silhouetted against the clear blue sky like giants gathered together in conversation. But Ma wasn't thinking of beauty. Her mind was fixated on what she planned to do next and as she went over the plan for the umpteenth time, she also prayed to God, asking Him to help her achieve her objective . . . even though that objective, she knew, was not what God would have wanted her to do.

19

With Ma and Noah gone, there was no one to disturb Nash, and save for the sweltering heat he'd had a productive day.

For some time now he'd been trying to teach himself to use his right hand. It wasn't easy, but he was gradually getting better. With his left hand he wrote:

I am Sobek, who dwelleth amid his terrors. I am Sobek, and I seize my prey like a ravening beast. I am the great Fish which is in Kamui. I am the Lord to whom bowings and prostrations are made in Sekhem. And the Osiris Ani is the lord to whom bowings and prostrations are made in Sekhem.

Changing the pen to his right hand, he copied the verse again. The result pleased him: his writing was definitely improving. Satisfied, he leaned back, stretched — and froze.

Someone was coming. He could hear the unmistakable roar of their outboard motor. Rising, he went to the window and looked through the bars. Shortly a sleek white skiff appeared out of the swamp and headed for the Guidry dock.

Nash recognized the boat immediately and tensed. If Deputy Doucet was paying them a visit it could only mean trouble.

⋆ ⋆ ⋆

Insects whining about his ears, Deputy Doucet tied up his skiff and stepped onto the dock. Surprised not to see Ma Guidry sitting on the front porch, he hitched up his belt and shifted the weight of the gun on his hip. Noah wasn't around to greet him either. That too was unusual. Deciding they must be out back somewhere, the lawman plodded up the slope to the house.

He'd spent a long, hot afternoon questioning the locals about the Bayou

Butcher. His inquiries had proved fruitless until he'd finally stopped at Leblanc's store for a Dr Pepper.

He'd sat there for a while, drinking his soda and watching Leblanc tie one of his fancy flies for a customer before finally saying: 'I'm a nightcrawler man, myself. Don't have the patience for tyin' flies.'

Without looking up, Leblanc said bluntly: 'An' I got no patience with a man don't spit out what he' nosin' after.' He cut off some twine and looked questioningly at the Deputy.

Coming to the point, Doucet said: 'Know anyone around here who wears a necklace made of alligator teeth?'

Leblanc pondered the question for a moment. The cluttered store was quiet but for the buzzing flies and the rattling hum of an old White-Westinghouse refrigerator against the back wall.

At last Leblanc said: 'No wonder that Butcher *merde* still runnin' free. You people graspin' at straws, ain't you? Askin' after 'gator teeth and latex gloves.'

'Latex gloves? Who was askin' about them?'

152

'One of them FBI folks, the young feller with the ponytail like mine. He showed up here a few days ago, wantin' to know if I carried any. Ain't you boys got any *real* clues to go on?'

Doucet breathed on his mirror sunglasses and wiped them clean on his sleeve. 'What did you tell him?'

'Said I took 'em on consignment. Said when they didn't sell, I returned 'em — all but one box that I figured got left behind. 'Cept I was wrong. They didn't get left behind. I remembered later that I sold 'em.'

'Don't suppose you remember who to?'

'Sure I do. Ma Guidry.'

'What the hell did Ma want 'em for?'

'That diesel generator of hers. Is older than the mountains, an' she's always havin' to fix it. Guess she was sick of gettin' oil and grease on her hands.'

'The gloves — remember what brand they were?'

'That's what the FBI fella wanted to know. They was Gripp. They were thin and flimsy, an' I'll *never* stock them again.'

Deputy Doucet smiled to himself.

The lab has narrowed the gloves he wears down to two brands, Usave and Gripp.

And then —

We know he's young and fit, we know he's local, that he's left-handed, and wears size ten boots.

That pretty much described Nash Guidry — except that Nash hadn't lived around here for several years. Or had he? Ma had said that Nash was away at university. She'd told him that whenever he asked about Nash. But now that he thought about it, she'd never mentioned which university he was at.

Could it be that he sneaked home whenever he got an urge to kill? Or, maybe he wasn't at university at all. Maybe he was hiding in the swamp somewhere and Ma, who protected her boys like a jealous hen, was covering up for him?

Deputy Doucet drained his soda and set the can before the old storekeeper. 'Be seein' you, Jean.' He left.

Now, as he paused in front of the

house, he noticed that Ma's VW camper was missing and guessed that she and Noah had gone visiting. To make sure, he climbed onto the porch and hammered on the door.

There was no answer. He knocked again. Nothing. Damn. He'd wanted to get to the bottom of this today, not wait till morning. Then it hit him: the Guidrys' absence gave him a perfect opportunity to check around inside and see if he could find anything to substantiate his suspicions about Nash.

He knew that without a warrant legally it would be considered breaking and entering, and any evidence he found would be inadmissible. But a little recon wouldn't hurt. Besides, if Nash *was* the Butcher, this way he'd know in advance and could call in backup when he later arrested him.

And when that happened, man, would he enjoy seeing the look on the Feebees' faces!

He tried the front door. It was locked. That, in itself, was unusual. Most Swampers didn't bother to lock their doors. He tried the window. It was locked too. Going around in back, he opened the broken screen door and tried the kitchen door behind it. It was locked, but easily opened under his push.

He entered the dismal little kitchen. Looking around, he saw a sink, a wooden table surrounded by ladder-back chairs, a chugging refrigerator edged with rust, cupboards and a bulky propane-fed Magic Chef stove. Seeing nothing suspicious, he went into the hall. It was littered with trash that Ma had never bothered to throw out. Wrinkling his nose at the stench, he went upstairs and entered the first bedroom he came to. It was Ma's. After a quick look around, he moved on to the room at the end of the hall. Unlike the other rooms, the door was closed. He eased it open and peered inside. The curtain was pulled, dimming the bedroom. He entered cautiously, crossing the thin white line chalked on the floor without noticing it, and saw a bowl and pitcher on top of a chest of drawers . . . a single closet . . . a bookshelf . . . and running along the left-side wall, a single unmade bed.

Someone was in the bed, covered by a blanket. As he walked toward it, he heard a weak cough. A moment later one of the Guidry twins sat up, startled to find Deputy Doucet in front of him.

'Wh-what you doin' here, Sheriff, huh, huh?'

Recognizing Noah's voice, Doucet apologized for waking him, then said: 'What's wrong with you, son? You ailin'?'

'Y-Yes, sir,' Nash said, mimicking his brother's voice and mannerisms. 'Got me a bad belly ache. Ma told me to stay in bed. She did. Honest. Said she'd fetch some medicine. You ain't sick too, are you?'

'No, I'm fine, boy.' Deputy Doucet paused, trying to think of a reason to justify his presence. 'I . . . uhm . . . just stopped by to talk to your mom. Door was open so I come on in and . . . '

'Sure am thirsty,' Nash murmured.

'Want some water?'

'*Oui, oui, s'il vous plait.*'

Deputy Doucet went to the pitcher,

poured water into a glass and brought it back to Nash. He'd already decided that he'd let Noah drink his fill, put the glass back where he'd found it and leave. If Noah later told Ma that he'd been there, he'd simply deny it and put it down to the boy's fever-fed imagination.

Handing the glass to the sick man, he said: 'Better sit up, Noah. Don't want to spill this.' As he spoke, he kicked something that clanked. He looked down and saw a length of chain trailing out from under the blanket. Puzzled, he bent down to check on it when —

Nash slammed the glass in his face. The glass shattered. Stunned and bleeding, Doucet stumbled back. Nash was on him instantly. Both went sprawling. Quickly straddling the lawman, Nash wrapped the chain around his fist and began whipping the Deputy about the head. Doucet tried to protect himself with his hands, but it was useless. Nash hit him again and again. Groggy, the lawman reached for his gun. He managed to get the Glock out of the holster. But before he could fire it, Nash grabbed his wrist, forcing it upward.

The gun went off. In the muzzle-flash Doucet saw the face above him and realized the man trying to kill him was Nash, not Noah. Desperate, Doucet punched Nash with his free hand. Nash rocked back and kicked out, knocking the gun from the Deputy's hand. It skittered across the floor.

Doucet tried to scramble for it, but Nash punched him with his chain-wrapped fist. Doucet collapsed. Nash pounced on him, pinning him with his knees. Then quickly unwrapping the chain from his fist, he looped it around the Deputy's neck and jerked it tight.

Doucet struggled for a few moments and then went limp.

Exhilarated, Nash continued to choke him long after the Deputy was dead. Finally, his need to kill satiated, he dropped the chain and he looked around for the gun.

It lay behind the door — just on the other side of the chalk line.

Getting off the body, Nash crawled as far as the chain allowed, stretched his arm out and tried to grasp the gun. It was just out of reach.

Rising, he took the blanket off the bed and threw one end over the Glock. He then gently pulled it toward him. It was no good. The blanket wasn't heavy enough to drag the gun back with it. Frustrated, he looked around for something else to use, but saw nothing. He'd have to wait until Ma and Noah came back from wherever they'd gone . . . and hope he could get his brother to get it for him before Ma found it.

20

For Ma, driving in New Orleans was a nightmare. Everywhere she looked she saw traffic, people, tall buildings, construction work, chaos. Noah must have felt the same way because he started whimpering.

She kept driving until she reached Baronne Street. The Plaza towered over them, big and square, its white-stone façade covered in row upon row of windows and balconies. She looked for a parking space out front. There wasn't any, only valet parking, and she couldn't afford that. She drove around the block again, still looking for a space. On her third try someone finally pulled out, and Ma quickly claimed the spot.

Dusk had fallen, making the city even more alien to her. Having seen a payphone at the last intersection, she told Noah to stay put and got out of the camper.

Noah immediately panicked. 'Where you goin'?'

'I got to make a call. Don't worry, I won't be long.'

'Can't I come with you? Huh, Ma? Can't I?'

'No. You just stay right here.'

'Promise you won't leave me?'

'I won't leave you, son.'

She lumbered back along the narrow sidewalk until she reached the payphone. As she dug into her frayed bag for the number of the Plaza Hotel, her fingers touched Peyton's old .45. The thought of what she was going to do next made her feel sick. But there was no going back now.

She called the hotel and asked to speak to Dr Ward. The operator put her through and a moment later a young girl's voice said: 'Hello?'

'Can I speak to Dr Ward?' Ma asked cautiously.

'My dad's not here,' said Chelsea.

Ma's heartbeat quickened. 'When will he be back? I . . . I got a package for him.'

'Do you want to bring it up? I'll take it.'

Ma couldn't believe her luck. 'What's your room number?'

'Six-three-two.'

'Merçi.'

Ma hung up.

★ ★ ★

Elliott had taken Kate to a restaurant in the heart of the French Quarter. After the maitre d' seated them and handed out menus, Kate asked about Chelsea. 'If she's not feeling well, are you sure you still want to have dinner? I mean, we could just have a quick drink and — '

Elliott chuckled. 'Believe me, she'll be fine. Truth is, I don't think she's sick at all.'

'Just wanted to avoid me, right?'

'On the contrary, she said you're cool. High praise indeed from my daughter. No,' he went on, amused, 'I think she wanted us to be alone.'

'God, what did you tell her about me?'

'Just that you wanted to jump my bones, and threatened to have me investigated if I didn't succumb to all

163

your perverted desires.'

'Got that right, buddy boy.'

'You know,' he said, 'I really can't believe we're together again. There were times, many times when I didn't think we'd ever see each other again.'

'Me, too.'

A waiter came and took their drink order.

'How's it going with your investigation?'

'Good. We're actually starting to make progress.'

'Anything you can talk about?'

'Not right now.'

He grinned ruefully. 'Then I guess this conversation's going to be pretty one-sided.'

'Oh, I dunno. There are plenty of things to talk about besides my work.'

'You're right,' he said, taking her hand. 'I want to know everything about you. Where you live, what you do when you're not working, do you have a boyfriend, have you been married — '

'Whoa, whoa,' Kate said, laughing, 'one question at a time, please.'

'All right, do you have a boyfriend?'

'No. Don't look so surprised,' she said. 'Lately, I haven't even had time for myself, let alone someone else.'

'That's right,' Elliott remembered. 'But for your 'personal advisor,' you wouldn't be here with me tonight. Who is it, by the way? I'd like to thank them one day.'

'My partner, Rosy.'

'You must think a lot of her to take her advice.'

'She's a he — Rosy's short for Rosario. And yeah, I do think a lot of him. We've had each other's backs for years now. Gets so you rely on each other. Think for each other. Finish each other's sentences. Worry about each other — '

'Love each other?' Elliott threw in.

Kate frowned, as if the thought had never occurred to her. 'Am I in love with Rosy — that what you're asking?'

'Are you?'

'Sure. But not in the way *you* mean. He's always there for me. Oh, I could strangle him sometimes but — ' She paused as the waiter brought their drinks.

When he was gone, Elliott held up his glass in mock toast. 'To Rosy,' he said, 'for bringing us together.'

Kate laughed. 'Be careful what you wish for . . . ' They clinked glasses and drank. 'Before we go any further, Elliott, there's something I'd like to ask you.'

'Am I ready for another relationship?' He laughed as she looked surprised. 'Don't worry. I can't read minds. It's just that I've been asking myself that same question ever since Atlanta, when I watched you drive away.'

'And . . . ?'

'You know how much I loved Shannon. No one could ever take her place. After she died . . . my whole world fell apart. Losing her like that, you know, so unexpectedly, I . . . well, if I hadn't had Chelsea, I don't know what I would've done.'

'I'm sorry. I didn't mean to open up old wounds.'

'You haven't. In any case, it's true what they say. Time *does* heal. And to *finally* answer your question, yes — I think there *is* room in my life for another woman now, someone who'd be willing to take me and Chelsea as a package and could handle having to share her life with a control freak.' He grinned sheepishly. 'Does that sound like I'm campaigning?'

'Not to me. But then I've always had the hots for you.' When he frowned, surprised, she said: 'Good God, Elliott, you must have known how I felt.'

'I knew you liked me — '

'*Liked?*' Lowering her voice, she leaned across the table and said: 'I fuck my best friend's fiancé and all you can come up with is *liked?*'

'I meant you didn't do anything about it.'

'What *could* I do? Shannon and I were like sisters. She used to pour her heart out to me all the time about how she'd die if she didn't marry you. What was I supposed to say to stuff like that? Besides, other than that afternoon, which I put down to varsity rutting season, you never gave me any reason to believe you loved anyone but Shannon.'

'That's not to say I didn't wonder how it would be with you. I did. *Often.*'

'You did a great job hiding it.'

'It's like you just said. What else *could* I do?'

Having no answer, she buried herself in the menu without reading the items.

'Is that the reason you didn't call me after Shannon died?' he asked.

'Yes. And now I wish I'd stayed away for good.'

He started to say something. But she was too upset to listen anymore. Throwing down the menu, she grabbed her purse, got up and hurried out.

Startled, Elliott didn't react for a moment. Then he tossed some money on the table and ran after her.

Outside, he waved off the valet parking attendant and in the darkness saw Kate hurrying toward the intersection.

'Kate! Wait!'

She didn't answer; didn't even look back.

He ran after her, grabbed her by the arm and swung her around to face him.

'Let me go, Elliott!'

'Not until I tell you something,' he said. 'You think you're the only one who got hurt by what happened back then? Jesus, you don't know the *half* of it.'

'I know that you fucked me and then

forgot all about me,' she said.

'Is that what you think? That all I was interested in was your *body?*'

'Weren't you?'

He sighed, let go of her arm and offered her his hand. 'Let's walk,' he said wearily.

She hesitated, emotions churning, and then took his hand. It was full dark now and as they walked, the streetlights striped the sidewalk with their shadows. They reached a corner and turned down Bienville Street. Like the rest of the French Quarter, it was narrow and lined on both sides with buildings painted in bright colors.

'You know, the weird thing is,' Kate said presently, 'I've rehearsed this moment a hundred times in my head. We'd bump into each other while I was on a case, I'd find out that you loved me like I loved you and we'd both live happily ever after. 'Course, deep down I knew I was kidding myself. Whether Shannon was alive or dead, you couldn't care less about me. You made that plain enough at the time. But it was my fantasy, so I went for it. And now here we are, together again, and suddenly I can't decide if I really do love you or if I'm just in love with the *idea* of loving you, and trying to find closure.'

They walked on in silence for a while. Then he stopped and turned her toward him. 'All right, Kate Palmer,' he said. 'You've had your say. Now I'll have mine. And then perhaps we can get on with our lives.'

She waited, wondering if after all these years his words would still mean anything.

'You're right,' he admitted. 'As far as I was concerned, you were always just Shannon's friend Kate — until that night I saw you toweling yourself off. When I saw you like that, naked, I wanted you. God, I wanted you so badly I could almost *taste* it — '

'Well, you didn't have to wait long till you got what you wanted,' she said bitterly.

'That was the problem, Kate. I got more than I bargained for that afternoon. Afterwards, I realized that it wasn't just your body that I wanted, it was *you, all* of you.'

'Ha,' she said. 'Next come the violins.'

'I'm serious. Don't you get it, even now? I discovered feelings for you that afternoon that I had no right to have, and they scared me. I felt ashamed afterwards, not because of what we did but because of how I *felt*. I was with Shannon. We were in love — *engaged*, for chrissake. How could I be in love with her best friend at the same time?'

She frowned. 'So that's why you ignored me afterwards?'

'I had to. I couldn't trust myself to do anything else.'

She felt a sudden flush of relief, that he hadn't just used her after all. But for some reason she couldn't let him off the hook. 'How do I know you're not lying?' she said.

He jerked her around to face him. 'Look at me,' he said, forcing her to meet his gaze. 'Do I look like I'm lying?'

Kate looked into his eyes and saw nothing but honesty.

'God, you're adorable,' she said. Cupping her hands about his face, she pulled his mouth close and kissed him.

Just then her cell phone buzzed. Elliott heard it too and instinctively held her tighter. 'Don't,' he said as she reached for it. 'Ignore it.'

She wanted too, more than anything. 'I can't,' she said.

'Please.'

'Sorry . . . ' She slipped out of his arms, dug out her cell, checked the caller ID and said: 'I've got to take this.' Then, as he sighed, frustrated: 'Why don't you give Chelsea a buzz and see how she's doing? I know you're worried.'

She answered her phone and said: 'Go ahead.'

Les Field, the senior CSI from the St Tammany Parish Sheriff's Office, said: 'I hope this isn't a bad time.'

'Uh, no,' she lied.

'I just got the last of the test results back from everything we lifted from the Gaspard place.'

'And?'

'It's not good, Agent Palmer. We've got plenty of stuff that'll convict your man when you catch him, but nothing that will help you do that.'

'Too bad,' she said. 'What about those traces of alloy steel and zinc plating? Anything on those yet?'

'Nothing so far. My guess is that they come from some sort of hardware — a key, a chain, wire, anything made of metal. Zinc plating protects metal by preventing rust, but since we haven't been able to match it with anything at the crime-scenes, we have to assume it was brought in from elsewhere.'

Just then Kate was distracted by the sudden urgency she heard in Elliott's voice.

'Chelsea?' he said loudly. 'Chelsea, are you there? Answer me, will you, sweetheart?'

Realizing that something was wrong, Kate said: 'I gotta go, Les. Thanks again.' She ended the call and turned to Elliott. 'What is it? What's wrong?'

His expression said plenty.

21

Earlier, Chelsea had been curled up in an armchair, watching *Survivor* on TV while she talked on her cell phone.

'Hot dogs, s'mores and beer at the lake? Oh God, Cheryl, I hate you for having so much fun while I'm stuck here in this — ' The phone beeped, signaling another call. 'Hold on. That'll be my dad checking to see if I've burned the place down yet or decided to get it on with the guy from Room Service . . . No, actually he's really hot. I saw him in the hall and . . . No, 'course I wouldn't, but dad doesn't know that. Wait, I'll be right back.'

She punched the call-waiting button and said: 'Hi, Dad. Yeah, yeah, I'm fine . . . What? . . . Not yet, no . . . 'Cause I wasn't hungry. But I've already called Room Service and — '

As if on cue, the door buzzer sounded. 'That's probably him now. Hang on.'

She set the phone on the arm of the chair, rose and went to the door. Opening it, she said: 'Come in. I'm on the phone, but — '

She broke off, startled, as she realized it wasn't Room Service.

Instead, she found two strangers staring at her: one an impossibly fat, homely woman in a soiled brown dress and broken-down shoes, the other an unkempt, shabbily-dressed man, maybe thirty, with curly, fairish hair and vacant, deep-set eyes that didn't quite match.

'Y-Yes?' she said, puzzled.

Ma Guidry sized her up. 'You are *le docteur's* daughter, *oui?*'

'Sure,' Chelsea said. 'Are you the one who's got my dad's package?'

Instead of replying, Ma lunged forward.

*　*　*

In Kate's hotel room Elliott repeated: 'Chelsea? Chelsea, answer me! Are you there?'

Covering the mouthpiece, he turned to Kate. 'She's talking to the guy from

175

Room Service. I hope to Christ he's not cute or she'll probably forget all about me.'

Into the phone he said: 'Chelsea! Dammit, Chelsea, pick up!'

But Chelsea didn't pick up.

Instead, all Elliott heard was the sound of a struggle — followed by a muffled scream that he was sure came from his daughter.

22

As the elevator carried them up to the sixth floor, Elliott said irritably: 'I know what I heard, Kate.'

'You know what you *thought* you heard,' she said calmly. 'You were upset. You could have been mistaken.'

They'd already been through this in the cab from Bienville Street. And she was right. What he'd heard could have been anything. But Chelsea hadn't come back to the phone, and all he'd heard was the ominous silence of an empty room.

'You should've called reception like I asked,' Kate continued. 'Had the clerk send someone to check on her.'

'Yeah, right, and if she was there have her accuse me of checking up on her? No thanks.'

'Well, is this any different? Coming home early to check on her yourself?'

He knew she was right but he wasn't about to admit it. The door slid open.

They stepped out and hurried to his suite. He swiped the plastic key through the lock and opened the door. Inside, the TV was on but the living area was empty.

'Chelsea?'

No reply.

He crossed to her bedroom door and knocked. 'Sweetheart? You in there?' When no one answered, he opened the door and looked inside. 'Goddammit, where *is* she?'

'Elliott, calm down,' Kate said. 'She left the TV on, so she can't have gone far. Probably just went downstairs to buy a magazine.'

'No way. She knows my rule — never leave the room except in a hotel emergency.' Catching Kate's expression he added: 'She's only fourteen, for chrissake!'

'And you, of course, never broke *any* rules when you were that age, right? Look, you stay here in case she comes back or calls, and I'll go check out the lobby, see if anyone's seen her.'

As she left, Elliott noticed Chelsea's cell phone on the arm of the chair. He grabbed it, put it to his ear. The line was dead. He caught up with Kate at the elevator.

'Something's definitely happened to her,' he said, alarmed. 'She'd never go anywhere without this.'

'Always a first time.'

'Don't patronize me, goddammit!'

'All right, I admit that it's unlikely. But losing your cool before we know she's in trouble isn't the answer, so just calm down, okay?'

The elevator arrived. Kate stepped inside, turned and said firmly: 'Go back to your suite, Elliott. I'll handle this. It's what I'm trained to do.'

The elevator doors closed and he was left all alone.

★ ★ ★

But it soon became obvious that he was right to be worried. Chelsea wasn't in the lobby or the restaurant; no one had seen a girl fitting her description; and a quick check revealed that the room had been empty when her Room Service order arrived.

While Elliott sweated in grim silence, Kate called the New Orleans Police Department. She was still on the phone when two detectives from the General Assignments Unit showed up fifteen minutes later.

They were large, tight-lipped men who wasted no time getting to the point. The one who introduced himself as Lieutenant Walker did most of the talking while his partner, a black detective named Groves, took notes.

'And you say your daughter went to answer the door and you heard her scream?'

'I heard what I *took* to be a scream, yes.'

'Then you couldn't swear to it?'

'Well . . . no. It was muffled, indistinct.'

'Do you know anyone in New Orleans, Dr. Ward?'

'No.'

'You weren't expecting visitors, then?'

'No.'

'Can you think of any reason why she would have left the room?'

'No. I already told you. Chelsea

180

wouldn't go anywhere, especially without her cell.'

'Was she upset about anything?'

' . . . No.'

'With respect, doctor, you don't sound too sure about that.'

'Well, she wasn't upset, exactly. But . . . '

'Go on.'

'My wife — Chelsea's mother — died in an automobile accident about a year ago. Things have been a little . . . strained between us ever since. She didn't really want to come on this trip, but New Orleans was to be our last stop. Another couple of days and we were going back to New York.'

Kate ended her call and joined them. 'I just gave your captain Chelsea's description and he's putting out an A.P.B.,' she told the detectives.

Lieutenant Walker gave her a cool glance. 'Am I to assume that the FBI is taking over this case?'

'No. But Dr Ward is a friend of mine. And what you *can* assume is that I'm going to do everything I can *personally* do to help him find his daughter. Do you have a problem with that, Lieutenant?'

'No, ma'am. Just wondering why the FBI is getting involved in a simple runaway.'

'Damn you!' Elliott exploded. 'My daughter *didn't* run away!'

Kate put a restraining hand on his chest and felt his heart thudding under his shirt. 'Cool down,' she told him. 'Everything that can be done is being done. All we can do now is wait and hope that Chelsea contacts you.'

'Does your daughter have a boyfriend?' asked Detective Groves.

'No.'

'You're sure?'

'Reasonably sure.'

'No one she's mentioned more than once?' said Walker.

'I've told you.'

'What about the internet? Does she use any of the social networking sites?'

'I don't know. Probably.'

'In any of the other cities you lectured, did you notice anyone hanging around your hotel or following you?'

'No.'

'They wouldn't necessarily look suspicious, just another face in the crowd. Think, doctor. It could be important.'

'No one that I can remember,' Elliott said. His eyes narrowed as something occurred to him. 'Are you saying Chelsea's been kidnapped?'

'I'm saying it's a possibility we can't discount,' Lieutenant Walker said carefully. 'Hotel this size, it wouldn't be hard to sneak someone out the back in, say, a linen cart.'

It seemed so specific that Kate said: 'What makes you say that, Lieutenant?'

Walker shrugged. 'According to one of the maids, someone stole her cart earlier this evening and left it in the alley behind the hotel.'

'No . . . ' Elliott swayed and Kate quickly steadied him. 'Oh Christ, no!'

23

After the two detectives left there was nothing to do but wait, and as always waiting proved to be the toughest job of all. Kate watched Elliott pace the floor until she couldn't stand it any longer. 'Park it, will you?'

He stopped. 'What'd you say?'

'Sit down. You're wearing out the carpet.'

He sank into a chair opposite her, but couldn't relax.

Kate didn't blame him. An investigation was already in progress. Even now traces of DNA found in the abandoned laundry cart were being analyzed to see if they matched that belonging to Chelsea, and the hotel staff was being questioned.

Deciding a drink might help calm his nerves, she went to the mini-bar.

'Is it true what they say?' asked Elliott. 'That kidnappers rarely let their victims go?'

'Elliott,' Kate said firmly, 'listen to me. First, we don't know yet if Chelsea *has* been kidnapped, and second, each kidnapping is different and has to be handled accordingly. Now, I know it's hard, but until we find out exactly what's going on, there's no point in jumping to conclusions.'

He drew a shaky breath. 'You must think I'm a jackass.'

'No,' she said gently. 'I think you're a father who loves his daughter very much.' As she handed him a Scotch, the phone rang. They looked at it for a moment, neither moving. Then Kate answered it.

'Dr Ward's suite.' Seeing Elliott's expression, she shook her head: it wasn't Chelsea. 'Who's calling, please? . . . All right, I'll put him on.' She pressed the privacy button. 'It's a woman,' she told him. 'Wants to talk to you. Won't give her name.'

He was up and reaching for the phone immediately, but Kate held it out of reach. 'Play this carefully, Elliott. Don't lose your temper and start threatening her. Promise her whatever she wants and don't do anything to antagonize her.'

He nodded and she handed him the phone. 'Wait until I pick up the extension.' She hurried into the bedroom and lifted the phone there. 'Okay,' she called out.

Forcing himself to be calm, he released the privacy button and said: 'This is Elliott Ward. Who is this?'

'We spoke this mornin',' said Ma.

Elliott cursed. 'Look, I told you not to call this number — '

'I got your *jeune fille,*' said Ma. 'And unless you help me, I kill her.'

He sagged. Kate hissed to him from the bedroom doorway. *Ask her what she wants.*

'W-What do you want?' Elliott asked.

'You know what I want. I got me a son. He one smart boy but sometimes he can be *tres dangereux*. You operate on him, like you say on TV, an' fix his brain, *oui*? Then I give you back your daughter.'

'I can't do that. I told you that this morning.'

'Well, that's what you gonna have to do if you want her back.'

'I want to speak to her.'

'No.'

'Put her on.'

Silence.

'I need to know that she hasn't been harmed.'

'She ain't. Yet.'

'I want *her* to tell me that.'

Ma sighed, clearly angry. 'You operate, you get your *jeune fille* back in one piece. Agreed?'

'It's, uh ... not that simple. The surgery's still in the experimental stage. I can't guarantee what the results will be.'

'You say on TV that *l'opération* would be successful. You told me yourself it would.'

'It will — one day. Right now I can't promise that your son will be cured or if he'll even survive the surgery. He could just as easily die under the knife.'

There was a long, empty pause. Then:

'You say this to scare me, but I don't scare. You say yes to *l'opération, Docteur,* an' next time I call, you tell me which hospital to bring my boy to. *Comprendre?*'

Before he could reply the line went dead.

Kate slowly replaced the phone, her mind already shifting gears, considering options, avenues to explore, possible outcomes. After a moment she rejoined Elliott.

'You spoke to this woman earlier?'

'She called right out of the blue. I thought she was a crank.'

'And you never thought to mention it when the cops were here?'

'I didn't think it was important. Truthfully, I'd forgotten all about it.'

'Did she give you her name?'

'No.'

'Did she tell you where she was calling from? Think, Elliott!'

'No, dammit! I asked her who she was but she just kept talking and didn't say.'

Kate turned from him, but not before he saw her expression. 'What is it?' he demanded.

'Nothing. Don't worry, Elliott. We'll get Chelsea back, I promise.'

'How? You heard her. She wants an operation for some psycho kid she's got — an operation that's only ever been performed on animals! What happens if

188

it goes wrong and I kill her precious son — ?'

'It's not going to come to that,' Kate said firmly. 'So long as she thinks she's got the upper hand, Chelsea's safe.'

Excusing herself she took her cell into the bathroom. When she came out again a few minutes later she said: 'I just filled my boss in on what's happened. Since I'm already involved he's agreed to let me handle the case.'

'Can you do that? Just waltz in and take over from the cops?'

'You let me worry about that.' She keyed in another number, waited a moment, and said: 'Rosy? I'm at the Plaza, Dr Elliott Ward's suite. I want you to arrange a tap for his telephone, *pronto*.'

'You got it. Anything else?'

'We've got a Cajun woman, judging from her accent, in her fifties, maybe, heavyset, lungs in bad shape. She says she's got a son who's dangerous, and she's demanding that Dr Ward perform an operation that she believes can moderate psychopathic behavior.'

Rosy was quiet for a very long moment.

Finally he said: 'Coincidence?'

'I don't believe in coincidence any more than you do.'

Elliott, who'd been listening to her end of the conversation, grabbed Kate's arm and spun her around. 'Coincidence? What's a coincidence? What's going on, Kate?'

Meeting his eyes, she said into the phone, 'Arrange it, homey,' and ended the call.

'I want an answer,' Elliott said. 'I want to know what you meant by 'coincidence.'' Even as he spoke it dawned on him. 'Oh-my-God, are you saying Chelsea's disappearance is connected to your serial killer case?'

Kate hesitated. 'Maybe,' she said softly.

'Jesus-Fucking-Christ, Kate, you told me I didn't have to worry about bringing Chelsea to New Orleans! You said your 'problem' was in the bayous east of here!'

'It is. And we don't yet know for sure that there really is a connection.'

'But you think it is, right?'

'It's one possibility, yes. We've got a psycho out there who makes Ted Bundy look more like Walt Disney. We've got three sets of victims who've all been Cajun. And now we get a woman with a Cajun accent telling us that her boy's dangerous — which could mean homicidal — and asking for an operation she believes can moderate psychopathic behavior.'

Elliott frantically ran his fingers through his hair. 'Dammit, Kate, how could you?'

'I'm sorry,' she said. 'But until I know differently that's the way I'm reading it. So if it makes you feel better to blame me for Chelsea's abduction, be my guest. But every second I stand here taking pies in the face from you is another second I'm not closing in on the kidnapper.' She met and held his gaze. 'Now, do you want to vent some more, or should I round up a task force?'

Elliott glared at her for another moment, and collapsed in a chair.

'Good call,' Kate said. 'We've a lot to do. First of all I need to speak to the nearest CARD team.'

'CARD?'

'Child Abduction Rapid Deployment. They deal with this kind of situation every day.'

'And then?'

'We need to find a hospital so you can perform the operation.'

'I *can't* operate,' he said. 'It's too risky.'

'*You* know that,' she said, 'and *I* know that. But the kidnappers don't. And you better pray they never do.'

24

Ma parked her VW camper beside the house, squeezed out from behind the wheel and looked at Noah, still in the passenger seat. 'Listen carefully now. Give girlie some water but don't untie her. Not for no reason. You got that, son?'

Noah nodded eagerly. 'Sure, Ma. Don't untie her. Not for no reason. I can remember that. Honest.'

Ma climbed onto the porch, every step an effort, unlocked the door and entered the house. Exhausted, she waddled into the kitchen and turned on the light. Intending to fix herself some coffee and then rest for a while, she froze as she saw something that chilled her blood.

The screen door was shut, but the kitchen door was ajar, and she knew that she had shut it before she and Noah had left for New Orleans.

She thought: *Nash. Mon Dieu, he's escaped again . . .*

Hurrying from the kitchen, she lumbered along the dark narrow hall. Not even pausing to switch on the light, she labored up the rickety stairs, yelling Nash's name as she went. She was gasping for air by the time she reached the hall, but she didn't stop to catch her breath. She didn't dare. If something had happened while she was gone and Nash had somehow gotten free —

She pushed his bedroom door wide open, flipped on the light. There was a body-shaped lump under the rumpled blankets, but she knew that could just as easily be a couple of pillows, arranged to make it look as if Nash were sleeping.

She entered the room, tempted for a moment to cross the chalk line before quickly deciding against it. 'Nash? Nash, that you, boy?'

Her voice was high, tense, scared.

The shape didn't move.

'Nash!'

Oh Lord, she thought, *Oh Lord somehow he's upped and gone and there's no telling what awfulness he'll commit* —

But then the blanket stirred and Nash sat up, squinting in the light. 'What is it?' he asked, pretending that he'd just woken up.

Her shoulders sagged with relief. Slumping against the doorframe, she shook her head. 'Nothin', son. Nothin'. We' home now, that's all. You go on back to sleep.'

He snorted. 'An' you woke me up jus' for that?'

Too tired to argue, she switched off the light, left the room and closed the door behind her.

Nash grinned in the darkness. She hadn't noticed the bullet-hole in the ceiling, and the door had hidden the fallen gun from her. That meant it was still his for the taking, once he figured out a way to reach it.

He lay there a moment longer, listening to the protesting floorboards as Ma clumped downstairs. Then he threw back the blanket, rolled off the mattress and peered under the bed. Just visible through the gloom was Deputy Doucet's body, where he'd hidden it.

★ ★ ★

In the back of the camper, Noah lifted Chelsea off the floor and set her down gently on one of the upholstered seats at the narrow Formica table. Next he carefully removed her gag and offered her a mug of water.

Chelsea's first instinct was to scream, but she knew that wouldn't get her anywhere and might only make things worse. As near as she could tell, they were out in the middle of nowhere, which meant that no one would hear her scream anyway.

Instead she drew an unsteady breath, grateful that the rag was no longer stuffed in her mouth. Noah held the mug closer to her and she drank sparingly.

'P-Please,' she said hoarsely. 'Let me go.'

'Can't. Ma says not to. Honest.'

'Then . . . at least untie me. I can't feel my arms.'

Noah hesitated.

'Please,' she begged. 'They're all numb.' When he didn't answer, she said desperately: 'You . . . you don't understand. If you take me back to my dad, he'll give you a lot of money.'

That seemed to penetrate. 'He will?'

'Sure. That's why you kidnapped me, wasn't it — to get money?'

Noah shrugged. 'I dunno. Ma don't tell me stuff like that. She just say to grab you, so I grab you. Want some more water? Huh? Huh?'

Chelsea shook her head. During the drive here she'd overheard enough to know that this overgrown idiot was her best chance of escape. The fat woman was tough, abrupt, determined. There'd be no dealing with her. But Noah . . .

Noticing how he was looking at her, she tried a new tack. 'Do you think I'm hot?'

Noah frowned and his mouth went slack. 'You got a fever?'

'No, I mean . . . cute. Pretty.'

Noah squirmed with embarrassment. Reaching out, he shyly stroked her hair. Though repulsed, she forced herself not to jerk away.

'You real pretty, that's f'sure. Real pretty.'

'Wanna kiss me?'

He looked away from her, at the darkness beyond the camper's windows.

'You *have* kissed a girl before, haven't you?'

He nodded emphatically. 'Once. Loretta Ainsell. Back of the church. Nash said it was okay. He did. Honest.'

'Nash?'

'My brother. Him'n me, we twins, only opposite. Like reflections in Peetre's Pond. You know Peetre's Pond?'

Chelsea shook her head.

'Me'n Nash used to go fishin' there all the time. It was fun. I liked it. Only now we don't go 'cause Ma keeps him — '

'Know what?' Chelsea said, knowing she had to work fast, before the old woman came back. 'I bet you're a *good* kisser.'

'Loretta said I bit her lip. I didn't mean to, but — '

'Untie me, and I'll let you kiss *me*.'

'Uh-huh. Can't. Told you. Ma'd give me a whippin'.'

'She'll never know. You can say I was gone when you got here.' Seeing that he

198

was at least considering it, she added persuasively: 'You untie me and I'll let you kiss me twice.'

Noah leaned close. His cheeks flushed. Chelsea could see that he was tempted. He glanced over one broad shoulder to make sure Ma was nowhere in sight, then leaned closer, his tongue wetting his lips expectantly.

Chelsea braced herself.

But at the last moment he panicked and pulled back, confused. Quickly he gagged her again and ran out.

This time Chelsea wanted to scream whether anyone could hear her or not.

★ ★ ★

Up in his room, Nash heard the muted sounds of their conversation. He couldn't make out what was being said or who was saying it. Noah often talked to himself and his turtle, but Nash couldn't remember his brother ever answering himself in a different voice. And there'd definitely been two voices. Which suggested someone else was in the camper with Noah. And if Nash hadn't known better, that someone sounded like a *girl*.

Puzzled, he wondered exactly where Ma had gone today.

He listened again. He hadn't imagined it. Noah was definitely talking to a girl.

Rising, he went to the window and peered down at the roof of the camper. He wondered who the girl was and what she was doing here. Was she for him? Ma's idea of a gift, maybe? Her way of trying to make amends?

No, that was too much to hope for.

Wasn't it?

He continued to watch the camper.

25

Kate woke early the following morning, rolled up off Elliott's bed and found Elliott himself exactly where she'd left him the night before, staring out the window at the gray, still-sleeping city. She asked him if he'd gotten any sleep and he gave a shrug that could have meant anything. 'I read an article somewhere once,' he said distantly, 'about Bud Abbott and Lou Costello.'

'The 'Who's On First' guys? My boss at the Academy was crazy about them. Had all their old movies on tape. Pretty funny stuff.'

But Elliott wasn't listening. 'Costello's daughter drowned in their swimming pool,' he said.

'Ouch.'

He turned and looked sadly at Kate. 'He never got over it. Blamed himself entirely. Said if he hadn't hit it big and been rich enough to buy a pool, she never would've drowned.'

'Ahh. So that's what's going on here.'

'What do you mean?'

'You're not content to blame yourself for Shannon's death. You want to pile Chelsea onto your back as well.'

'I did make her come with me.'

'And if you hadn't, and she'd drowned while water-skiing, that would've been your fault too, right? For *not* making her come?'

He gave another meaningless shrug.

'Well, that's just great!' Kate said angrily. 'Good Christ, Elliott, you can't take responsibility for all of life's fuck-ups. I know you're used to playing God with that scalpel of yours, but you can't take the blame for everything that happens. And you certainly haven't got the monopoly on angst.'

'What's that supposed to mean?'

'Nothing.'

'No, no, you can't say something like that and then expect to weasel out of it.'

Ignoring him, she went to the coffee Thermos and poured herself a cup.

Elliott followed her. 'You deliberately

opened up an artery and I want to know why.'

'Forget it,' she said. 'I was wrong. I'm sorry.'

'No, no, apology not accepted. Now, let's have it, Kate. I want to hear what you've got to say.'

She didn't answer. Adding sweetener to her coffee, she stirred it with a straw and took a sip.

'I'm waiting,' he said.

She looked at him, eyes wet with frustration. 'Ah, shit,' she said suddenly. 'I've got no right to criticize you, Elliott. We're too much alike. You want to set the world to rights, and so do I. But the sad truth is that no matter what we do or how long or how well we do it, we're never going to cure all the world's ills, and that's hard for people like us, because it's like admitting defeat.'

'We ought to accept our limitations — that what you're telling me?'

'Yes — No, goddammit. What I'm telling you is that we might be control freaks, but inside we're good people, trying to do good things. Trouble is, we're only human, and sometimes we forget that. I never realized it until last night, when I saw life pull the rug right out from under you.' She paused, her mind elsewhere, and did not return for several moments. 'When this is over,' she said finally, 'and we have this bastard in custody, I'm taking a break.'

'A vacation?'

'More like an extended leave of absence. I don't know what I'm going to do exactly, or when I'm coming back to work, but maybe we could spend some time together — you and Chelsea, of course.'

Elliott smiled wearily. 'I'd like that, Kate. I'd like it a lot. And I think Chelsea would, too.'

'Then — '

Someone knocked on the door. 'That'll be Rosy,' Kate said. She went to the door, opened it, ushered her partner in.

She introduced the two men. They shook hands, each sizing the other up. Elliott saw a lithe, light-skinned Puerto Rican with intelligent hazel eyes; Rosy saw a tall man who'd gone to pieces and was desperately trying to regain control of himself.

'Has the kidnapper called back yet?' Rosy asked Kate.

'Uh-uh.'

'*Bueno.* I've got the phone tapped and the front desk is covered. All calls to this room will be put through without question.'

'When will your wiretap guys get here?' said Elliott.

'They won't. The days of men with reel-to-reel tape recorders and head-phones are long gone, Doc. We're in the digital age now. We tap remotely, by computer. All it takes is one call to set it up.'

'You guys can do that?'

'Sir, you'd be surprised at what we can do. And if it makes you feel any easier, you've got the added advantage of having Kate here on the case. She's the best — '

The telephone jangled, startling them.

Elliott looked at Kate, who nodded. He hurried to the phone, punched the speaker button and said: 'Dr Ward speaking.'

For a moment there was silence. Then

Ma Guidry said in a low voice: 'Where do I bring my boy, *docteur?*'

Kate caught his eye and made a stretching gesture with her hands. Realizing she meant play for time, he said: 'I'm, uh, not sure yet. I'm having problems finding a hospital. Since I'm only licensed to operate in the State of New York, their insurance doesn't protect them from law suits — '

'You sayin' you can't help *mon fils?*'

'N-No, not exactly. It's just — '

'Then no more stallin', *docteur.* The name and address of *l'hôpital,* or I hang up, an' I don't call you no more.'

'No, no, don't hang up,' he begged. 'Please . . . I believe I have a location. Got a pencil and paper?'

They heard her fumbling around, the rustle of paper and her labored breathing into the mouthpiece, then: *'Oui.'*

He gave her the address of the hospital Kate had contacted the night before and waited while she wrote it down. 'My boy,' she said then. 'When do I bring him, *docteur?*'

'Today. I'll go over there now and wait for you.'

'*Trés bon*. But remember, Dr Ward. Any harm come to my boy an' you don't never see you' *jeune fille* again.'

'You think I don't know that?' he said. But Ma had already hung up.

Moments later Rosy's cell phone buzzed. He took the call, listened, and looked grim. 'Sorry, Doc. She wasn't on the line long enough to get a trace.'

Elliott could have wept.

★ ★ ★

'*Merci, m'sieur,*' said Ma, turning from the phone to Leblanc.

The storekeeper, who was taking inventory, said: '*C'est mon plaisir, madame*.' Closing his ledger, he added: 'Did Deputy Doucet come out an' see you last night?'

Ma frowned uneasily. '*Non*. Why should he?'

'He was in here askin' about latex gloves. You know. The gloves you bought from me when your generator was actin' up?'

'Why for he interested in gloves?'

'*J'sais pas.* Maybe he's not. I just wondered.'

26

On the eighth floor of St Catherine's Metropolitan Medical Center, administrator David Timmons gestured for Kate and Elliott to be seated. 'I knew you by reputation, of course, Dr Ward, so I was only too willing to cooperate.'

'Thank you, I appreciate that.'

'I've assembled an operating team. All they know at the moment is that we have some kind of, uh, 'VIP' coming in for surgery and that it's all very hush-hush. I've also cleared an O.R. for you. It's yours as long as you need it.'

'That's great,' Elliott said. 'The whole purpose of what we'll be doing today is to convince this woman that I've operated on her son. We'll treat him just like any other O.R. patient. He'll go through assessment and pre-op, be anesthetized and though I won't perform the surgery she wants, I'll do just enough to make it look right.'

Inside Ma's camper, Noah forked up a portion of scrambled eggs and gravy-soaked grits and offered it to Chelsea. She turned her head away.

Noah frowned. 'Why won't you eat?' he asked, concerned. 'Aint you hungry? Huh? Huh?'

Chelsea shook her head. She studied him, thinking how pitiful he looked, crouched beside her with a greasy old John Deere cap pulled low over his long sandy-blond hair. 'Have you, uh, thought any more about kissing me?'

'*Oui, oui*, I wanna kiss you,' he said shyly. 'Lots.'

Heart racing, she said: 'Then you'll help me?'

'Sure. Uh . . . help you how?'

'To get away from here.'

'Oh, yeah. Now I remember.' He beamed, showing big yellow teeth. 'You want me to untie you an' take you to your pa.'

'He'll pay you whatever you want.'

'He will?' Noah looked confused. 'Why?'

Chelsea wanted to scream. ''Cause he

209

loves me. Wants to get me back, safe and sound. Understand?'

Noah nodded, bothered by his thoughts. 'My Pa loved me . . . me *and* Nash . . . but then he went away and never come back. Is your Pa in prison?' he asked suddenly.

'No. He's a doctor, a surgeon. Right now he's in New Orleans and if you'll drive me there, he'll give you anything you want.' She hesitated briefly, then said: 'You do still want to kiss me, right?'

'Sure. Lots. But I don't know if Ma — '

'Forget Ma,' Chelsea said. 'This is between you and me.'

'Just you'n me?' He beamed again; then almost immediately looked troubled. 'Don't 'spect Ma would like that.'

'Sure she would. Wants you to be happy, doesn't she?'

'I 'spect so. Yeah. Yeah, she want for me to be happy.'

'Well, there you are, then.'

'How will I be happy?'

''Cause I'll take care of you,' Chelsea said. 'Look after you. You'd like that, wouldn't you?'

He gave her an eager, slack-jawed nod.

'Just you'n me,' he repeated. 'An' you lookin' after me. My, won't that be somethin' — '

He broke off as he heard his mother calling to him from the porch. 'Noah! Son, get in here!'

'That's Ma,' he said. 'I gotta go.'

'No,' Chelsea said desperately. 'No, don't go. Please. Not yet. Untie me first. Then we can start making plans.'

Noah chewed his lip. He wanted to make plans with her, even if he didn't remember what those plans were afterward. But when Ma called, he had to come running. That was a lesson he'd learned long ago and one of the few he had no trouble remembering.

'I gotta go,' he repeated. And before she could argue, he quickly replaced her gag and hurried out.

★ ★ ★

In the kitchen, Ma finished pouring compounded laudanum into the mug of coffee before her. The last time she'd used it on Nash he'd slept for twelve hours.

211

She hoped it would work as well now, because there was no way she could hope to transport him to *l'hôpital* in New Orleans unless he was unconscious.

Judging the right dose had been guesswork. Ma hoped that six drops would be enough — and not too much. She spooned in extra sugar to disguise its bitter taste and set the mug on a tray, next to a plate of eggs and grits, and yelled for Noah.

When he came shuffling in, she told him: 'Take this up to your brother an' stay with him till he finish everythin'. His food, coffee, everythin'. *Entendu?*'

'Aw, Ma, do I have to? I mean, you know Nash don't like no one watchin' while he eat'.'

'Do as I say, boy. An' don't you drop the tray, hear?'

'I won't, Ma. You see. I'll carry it just like Nash would. Honest to God.'

'An' remember what I told you. Don't say nothin' about that girl to your brother.'

'I won't, Ma. Honest.' Noah left.

As he trudged upstairs she heard him

muttering: 'Don't tell Nash 'bout the girl
. . . don't drop the tray . . . wait till he
finish . . . don't tell Nash 'bout the
girl . . . '

She shook her head, suddenly worn
down by the weight of it all. She closed
her eyes and whispered fervently: 'Stay by
my side, Oh Lord. Do not let Your servant
falter now.'

★   ★   ★

As soon as Noah crossed the chalk line
and set the tray down, Nash grabbed him
and said: 'Okay, moron — who's in the
camper?'

Noah's eyes saucered. 'Nobody. Honest
to God, Nash. Ain't nobody in there at
all.'

'*Menteur!*' Nash knocked the John
Deere cap off his brother's head. 'Now
tell me the truth or you'll be sorry.'

Noah picked up his cap and stood
there, cowering. 'I am, I am,' he
stammered. 'Honest, Nash.'

'You wouldn't know 'honest' if it hit
you in the face,' Nash said. 'Now, quit

lyin', *p'tit frère*, and tell me who you been takin' food to?'

Noah squirmed and refused to make eye-contact.

'Look at me, damn you,' Nash said, shaking him. 'I know you got someone down there. I heard her. So who is she?'

Noah glanced fearfully at the open door. 'Swear you won't tell Ma?' he whispered.

'I swear.'

Noah sat on the bed beside the tray, hugged his drawn-up knees, and started rocking agitatedly.

In mumbling spurts, he told Nash everything he could remember about his trip with Ma to New Orleans. Much of it he couldn't remember, or comprehend. Finally he looked at Nash, who was now standing at the barred window, staring at the VW bus.

'If Ma finds out you know 'bout the girl, she give me the whippin' of *ma vie.*'

'I already promised I wouldn't tell her,' Nash said. 'Now get out of here, so I can figure out what she's up to.'

He stared fixedly at the camper, as if

214

perhaps he could penetrate the roof and see the girl inside, and by just seeing her he would get the answers he sought.

'I told you to get out of here,' he snapped when he realized Noah was still sitting there, rocking restlessly. 'Go on, scram!'

'I can't, Nash. Honest. I gotta stay till you done eatin'.'

'Ma say that?'

'*Oui.*'

'Why's she care if I eat or not? Never cared before.'

'That ain't true. Ma loves you.'

'Sure — an' I got the welts on my back to prove it.'

'She whips me too. But that's 'cause she loves us, an' don't want us to end up bein' evil, like Pa.'

'Pa wasn't evil, you moron.'

'But he done a bad thing. He rob' that gas station.'

'That's 'cause Ma was always naggin' him about how we didn't have no money to live on. She forced him into it!'

'She never done no such thing!'

Nash angrily whirled around, causing

the chain at his ankle to clank. 'What the hell's wrong with you?' he demanded. 'Don't you remember anything?'

'Sure, sure, I remember,' Noah said, anxious to please. 'I remember lots of things.'

'Like what, for instance?'

'I dunno. What you want me to remember?'

Nash snorted, disgustedly. 'You're dumber than shit,' he said. 'Don't know why I even bother talkin' to you.'

Crushed, Noah hung his head. 'Want me to tell you what I remember?' Then, when Nash didn't reply: 'Pa's comin' home.'

Nash laughed cruelly. 'You're *bête comme une oie.*'

'No, I ain't,' Noah said. 'I ain't crazy an' I ain't no goose. It's the truth.'

'Who says so?'

'Deputy Doucet. I heard him. He told Ma. Honest. I did, I did. Says they's lettin' Pa out of prison.'

'Idiot! You must've dreamed it. Ma said Pa was never coming back.'

Noah started crying again.

'Aw, Jesus Mary and Joseph,' Nash

said. 'All right, all right, I believe you. Now stop crying and think. Close your eyes, little brother, and think back. Try to remember exactly what you heard Deputy Doucet say to Ma.'

Noah closed his eyes and desperately tried to remember. 'I'm tryin',' he said. 'Tryin' real hard, Nash. But . . . '

'But, what?'

'Kisses,' he said suddenly. 'I remember that all right.'

'Kisses? What're you talking about?'

'The girl. Said I could have two kisses.'

'Now I know you're crazy,' Nash said. 'Why would this girl want to kiss you at all, let alone twice?'

''Cause she likes me, Nash. Likes me lots. Said I could kiss her. First, once and then twice. She said that, Nash. She really did. Said she'd come'n look after me.'

'Look after you?'

'Uh-huh. But I wasn't to tell Ma.'

Suddenly it all made sense. 'But first you had to untie her an' let her go, right?'

'How you know that, Nash, huh? Huh?'

Nash said only: 'What happened next?'

'I tol' you. She say I could kiss her twice.'

'Did you?'

'N-No, 'course not.'

'What *did* you do?'

'Nothin'. I didn't do nothin', Nash. Honest. 'Cept tell her 'bout Peetre's Pond.'

'Peetre's Pond?'

'*Oui, oui.* You know, how you'n me usta go fishin' there an' then she said her pa was a famous ... uh ... a famous ... ' He groped for the word and finally found it. 'A famous surgeon, an' ... an' ... What's a surgeon, Nash?'

'A doctor who operates on you, dummy. Now shut up a minute an' let me think.'

Noah obeyed. But he was too agitated to just sit in silence. His gaze wandered. Noticing the mug of coffee on Nash's tray, he said timidly: 'Okay if I have some of your coffee?'

'Help yourself. But only one sip,' Nash cautioned, 'or you'll get all wired and Ma will yell at you.'

'Only a sip. Sure, I can remember that.

Honest to God. Just one little sip.'

He picked up the mug and took a loud slurp. The coffee tasted sweet. So sweet, in fact, that he gave in to temptation and took another sip. And since Nash was still looking down at the camper, he quickly sneaked another . . . and another . . .

27

Ma waddled out into the misty front yard and crossed to the camper. She was feeling nervous about what lay ahead, and her heart pounded uncomfortably. Had she not been so preoccupied, she might have glanced toward the dock and seen Deputy Doucet's still-moored skiff, which was just visible through the haze. But she didn't.

Chelsea watched Ma squeeze awkwardly into the camper. Ma tried not to acknowledge the fear in the girl's dull, frightened eyes. She took no pleasure in what she'd done. But it was a necessary evil and that's all there was to it. So what if the child knew fear for a short time? She was young, she'd get over it.

Wincing at the pain in her back, she bent and untied the rope around Chelsea's ankles. Chelsea said something to her, but the gag muffled the words.

Unable to understand her Ma untied

the gag. Chelsea took a deep breath, sucking in the damp dawn air and said hoarsely: 'What are you g-going to do to me?'

'I not plan to hurt you,' Ma said. 'Not if you behave an' do like I say.'

Grabbing Chelsea by the shoulders, she pulled her out of the camper. Chelsea's numb legs buckled. Ma hauled her to her feet and began to drag her across the yard toward the woodshed. To Chelsea it looked as if she was being transferred from one kind of prison to another.

Digging her heels in, she cried: 'No — !'

'*Oui,*' said Ma, struggling with her. 'You only be in there a short while, then when your daddy do like I say we let you go — '

Chelsea kicked her in the shin. Ma yelped and lost her grip. Chelsea twisted free and stumbled backward.

Ma grabbed for her, but Chelsea eluded her grasp and tried to run. For a few steps she was wobbly-legged and almost fell. Then as the life came back into her legs, she regained her balance and raced toward the surrounding woods.

Ma lumbered after her, but knew she'd never catch her. 'Noah!' she yelled. 'Noah! Get out here, *viens vite!*'

★   ★   ★

'Ma's callin' you,' Nash told his brother. He had seen everything happen from his bedroom window. Now, as he watched Ma laboring pathetically after the girl, he giggled. 'Run, you ol' tub of lard! *Courir! Courir!*'

Still giggling, he turned from the window and saw Noah standing behind him, head down, guiltily twisting the coffee mug in his big-knuckled hands.

The *empty* coffee mug.

'I didn't mean to drink it all, honest,' Noah said plaintively. 'I just took one little sip like you tol' me — '

'Liar,' Nash said.

'No, no, is true, I swear — '

'Shut up,' Nash said. His agile mind quickly identified a situation he could exploit. 'Is okay,' he said, softening. 'I'll cover for you — if you'll do something for *me*.'

Anxious to avoid Ma's whipping, Noah

quickly nodded. '*Oui, oui.* What? What?'

Nash pointed to the open bedroom door. 'Behind the door, on the floor, there's a gun. Get it for me.'

'A gun?' Noah's eyes bugged. 'Where from you get a gun, huh? Huh?'

'Relax, is just a toy.'

'Oh-h . . . ' Disappointed, Noah shuffled over to the door. Deputy Doucet's gun lay where it had come to rest the night before. Picking it up, Noah peered down the barrel. 'Looks real to me,' he said.

'Give it here, you stupid turd.' Nash snatched it from him. 'Now take that tray an' get out of here.'

'Ain't you gonna eat you' breakfast? Ma told me — '

'You eat it. I'm not hungry.'

And thinking again of Ma's mysterious hostage, Nash added silently: *Not for food, anyway.*

★ ★ ★

On reaching the woods, Chelsea had to slow down in order to weave between the dense stands of trees. Trailing roots

223

snagged at her feet, forcing her to jump over them, while clumps of lush green ferns slowed her progress even more. Underfoot the ground was mostly flat but waterlogged. It clung to her feet so that she seemed to be running in a dream.

Around her the mist-shrouded trees and brush had come to life with animal and bird-sounds, weird and unfamiliar chirps and yelps and snuffling growls that filled her with dread. Her pulse thudded in her ears. Over its pounding she heard the rasp of her heaving lungs, mingled with the painful gasp of every exhalation.

On she blundered, knowing that if she lost her balance now she wouldn't be able to use her still-tied arms to break her fall. Eyes half-closed as protection against the low-hanging branches that whipped her cheeks, she forced herself to blunder on.

All around her the bayou looked the same. She had no idea which direction to take, only that she must head away from her pursuer. The woods swept past in a smudge of browns, grays and greens. She saw a deadfall log across her path and forced herself to run faster in order to leap over it —

She landed on the far side, miraculously still on her feet . . . and, as she began to sink, realized with horror that she'd jumped into a quagmire.

She quickly sank up to her ankles in the sluggish mixture of water, mud and half-rotten plant material. With nothing firm underfoot, she swayed back and forth for a moment and then pitched forward onto her knees. Immediately they too disappeared beneath the scummy, duckweed-covered surface.

Keep still, she told herself. *The more you struggle, the faster you'll sink. Wait, get your breath, think this thing out . . .*

But even standing still she continued to sink slowly into the mire. She was already up to her thighs, and it held her with a clinging grip she couldn't hope to break, certainly not without the use of her arms.

She sank another inch. The quagmire made faint oozing sounds as it slowly swallowed her. She looked around, desperately trying to think of some way to save herself.

It was hopeless.

Then she heard her pursuer again, somewhere off to her left. She looked in that direction, no longer caring if they caught her and threw her into that spider-speckled old woodshed. At least she'd still be alive.

'Help! Please! Over here!'

Her scream was muffled by the thickening white mist. She listened, hoping to hear someone answer. But no one did.

'Please! Someone! Help me! I'm trapped . . . I can't get out . . . I'm *sinking!*'

More silence.

The mire was up to her waist now, and steadily pulling her deeper. 'Help me! Oh God, somebody help me! *Please!*'

Finally she heard someone lumbering through the brush toward her. She peered through the mist, trying to see who it was but the dense undergrowth and vine-tangled trees hid everything.

Whoever was approaching was close now. Again, Chelsea screamed for help. Moments passed. Then finally Ma plodded out of the trees. Exhausted, her fat

226

face flushed and sweaty, she hobbled closer and flopped down onto the deadfall.

'Please,' Chelsea begged. 'Please get me out of here.'

Ma studied her, lungs wheezing as she struggled to regain her breath. 'Serve you right, girl, if I let you die.'

'Please,' Chelsea repeated, fighting back tears. 'I wouldn't be in this mess if you hadn't kidnapped me!'

Ma felt a stab of conscience. 'I know what you thinkin', child. But you're wrong. Noah an' me, we ain't mean people. We just obeyin' the Good Lord's message.'

'If you believe in God,' Chelsea said, 'you wouldn't let me die.'

That hit home. Bracing herself against the deadfall, Ma leaned forward, her right arm outstretched.

At first the girl was just beyond reach. Then Ma finally hooked her fingers into Chelsea's sweater, gathered the material between them and pulled.

The wool began to stretch but Chelsea didn't move. Ma pulled harder, hoping that the sleeve wouldn't tear.

Still nothing happened. Finally Ma managed to grasp Chelsea's arm and jerked on it. Chelsea felt herself move in the mire. The next moment the vacuum seal around her broke and she was able to use her legs to help kick herself loose.

'Lay . . . flat . . . an' stay still,' Ma told her.

Chelsea obeyed.

Grunting from the effort, Ma continued to pull on Chelsea's arm. Slowly, Chelsea came closer. Finally she was close enough for Ma to grab her with both hands, and with one final heave she dragged the girl out of the quagmire.

★ ★ ★

As soon as Noah left, Nash sat on the bed and aimed the gun at the padlock holding the chain around his ankle. If he missed he could cripple himself for life. But wasn't he already as good as crippled by this chain and these four walls and a mother who wouldn't let him roam free to fulfill his goal?

Head back, eyes half-closed, he checked his aim one last time and squeezed the trigger.

As the gunshot shattered the silence, the chain jumped and rattled. When the smoke cleared, Nash saw that the padlock had buckled but not broken. Cursing, he fired again.

This time the padlock broke open. Ears ringing, Nash shouted joyfully. Reaching down, he pulled the chain from the twisted hasp and flung it aside. He was finally free —

Just then there was a loud crash of dishes downstairs.

Stuffing the gun in his pocket, he hurried from the room. Downstairs in the kitchen Noah was on his hands and knees, surrounded by broken crockery and spilled grits.

'You dumb shit,' Nash yelled. 'Can't you even carry — '

He stopped as Noah looked up and Nash saw how glazed and unfocused his eyes were.

'What's wrong with you?'

Noah shook his head sluggishly. 'Dunno,'

he managed. 'Tired . . . ' Closing his eyes, he slumped onto his side.

Nash shook him. 'Noah?'

'Gonna . . . go . . . sleep now . . . ' Noah murmured.

Puzzled, Nash peeled back his brother's eyelids. All he saw were the whites. He felt Noah's forehead. He had no fever. But something had to be wrong for him to have collapsed.

Then Nash remembered what Noah had said earlier. *I gotta stay with you till you get done eatin'.*

Nash got a nasty suspicion; a feeling of *déjà-vu*. He gazed at the mess on the floor again, looking for clues. The shards of broken mug caught his eye. Had there been something in his coffee? Had Ma been trying to drug him again?

He looked at Noah. Maybe if he splashed cold water on his face he could bring him around enough to get some answers —

He saw it then, on the sink; a small, near-empty brown-glass bottle. Picking it up, he read the smudged, faded label on which was scrawled *Tincture of Opium*.

Laudanum!

Nash grinned mirthlessly. *Damn her eyes,* he thought. Well, two could play at that game. But he had to move fast. He had lots to accomplish before Ma got back.

★ ★ ★

Ma was exhausted by the time she had padlocked Chelsea inside the woodshed. The girl's pleading grated on her nerves and the two shots she'd heard had further unnerved her. Like everyone else, she knew poachers operated in the swamp, but she didn't like it when they came so close to the house.

When she entered the kitchen she found Noah on his hands and knees, picking up pieces of shattered china, his John Deere cap pulled low over his eyes.

'*Mon Dieu!* Can't I trust you to do nothin' right?'

Nash, wearing Noah's bib-and-brace overalls and speaking in Noah's voice, looked around wretchedly. 'Sorry, Ma,' he blubbered. 'I try hard to do what you say.

I did, I did. Honest to God. The tray, she just slip out of my hands.'

He finished clearing up. Ma looked at the fragments of the coffee mug. 'Now I got to start over again,' she grumbled.

'Don't be mad at me, Ma,' Nash said, mimicking Noah's plaintive tone. 'Please. I done like you said. I stay with Nash till he finish his breakfast. Honest.'

'What about his coffee? Did he drink it all?'

'*Oui, oui.*'

'Don' lie to me, boy. Is too important.'

'I ain't lyin', Ma. Honest. He did. Every last drop.'

Ma sighed with relief. Reaching into her dress pocket, she dug out the key to Nash's chain. 'All right. Now I got to make sure he's asleep. If he is, you'll have to help me carry him downstairs.'

'Sure, Ma. I can do that.' Nash hesitated, as he'd so often seen Noah do, then: 'If you want, I can go up an' bring him down for you. I can carry him all by myself, y'know.'

He watched Ma think about it. He knew that if he was going to pull this off she mustn't see the broken padlock or the bullet-holes in the floor and ceiling.

She hesitated, wondering if she could trust him with the task. At the same time she knew she was in no condition to climb the stairs again, not after chasing that *bête copine* through the woods.

'Here,' she said at last, giving Nash the key. 'But make sure he be sleepin' 'fore you unlock the chain, you hear me?'

Nash nodded, bobbing his head foolishly. 'Sure, Ma. Sure. I can remember that.'

28

Gnarled hands fisted at his sides, Peyton Guidry splashed determinedly through the swamp. He'd been brooding ever since Bekah had warned him not to try to see his boys. He'd backed off because he wanted to avoid trouble. But he had rights. And the only thing that had kept him going through fifteen long years at Elayn Hunt was the knowledge that one day he'd be reunited with his beloved sons.

In prison it had been drummed into him that he had to confront life's problems; learn to understand them; search for ways to control or otherwise deal with them, be ready and willing to implement strategies and then review them to see if there was any room for improvement.

But while resting in the tree house overlooking Peetre's Pond he'd realized that only one word from that list made any real sense — *confront*.

So he'd set off to confront Bekah, to demand her respect, and to see his sons. If she was telling the truth and they really didn't want to see him again . . . well, that was their choice. He had to respect that. But he wasn't about to allow Bekah to speak for them. They were grown men now, able to speak for themselves.

He was almost to the house now. He could partially see it through the trees. It fueled his excitement. He picked up the pace — and was almost clear of the woods when he heard doors slam and an engine start up. Immediately he broke into a run, his Confederate gray coat flapping about him, murky water splashing around his feet. But he was too late. As he reached the clearing by the house he saw Ma's old VW camper driving off down the trail leading out of the swamp. Shading his eyes from the sun, he stared after it and was able to make out that Ma was driving and one of his boys was riding next to her.

Peyton stopped and angrily kicked the dirt. His confrontation with Bekah would have to wait. But if he was lucky he'd have his reunion with his other son right now.

The front door was locked, which surprised him, and he had to go around in back and shoulder open the kitchen door. Inside, familiar smells flooded his sense; smells he thought he'd forgotten. They brought back memories, not all of them good. He glanced around and grimaced. The place had never been a palace, but at least it had been clean when he lived here.

'Hey,' he yelled. 'Anyone home?'

The empty house seemed to absorb his words like a sponge, taking with them even the echoes. Disappointed, he decided to look around. Hopefully, he'd find some photos of his boys and see how they had grown up.

Finding no pictures in the living room, he headed upstairs. The door to the room he'd slept in after the marriage had finally broken down completely stood ajar. Entering, he noticed the bars on the window and wondered why the hell they were there. Then he saw his beloved books on the shelf and his anger melted away, replaced by a warm, mellowing feeling. He went to the shelf, ran his fingertips across them as if they were priceless artifacts.

He knew then that in his absence this had become Nash's room. Noah had never learned to read and had no interest in books. But Nash had always been bright and quick to learn. He swallowed, suddenly overcome by emotion, as he wondered if Nash had kept his books as a way of remembering him.

He was rubbing the tears from his eyes when he saw the chain lying like a dead snake beside the bed, the broken padlock beside it. He frowned. The two holes in the floor next to them looked like bullet-holes. He moved closer to the bed and suddenly became aware of a sickening stench. Deciding that a rat or some other vermin must have gotten trapped under the floorboards and died, he was about to check beneath the bed when he heard pounding outside. He went to the window and looked out. The noise was coming from the woodshed.

Puzzled, he left the room and hurried downstairs, out into the yard. The pounding was louder, harder now. Whoever was trapped inside seemed determined to break out. Wondering who it was, he grabbed an axe that stuck into a pile of firewood and warily approached the shed.

★　★　★

They were almost out of the swamp now. The air-conditioning in the old VW camper had long ago stopped working and Ma, her massive bulk squeezed behind the wheel, was bathed in sweat.

Beside her Nash did his best to keep his face turned from his mother. Under his John Deere cap his hair was parted to the right, like Noah's naturally was, and he was careful to mimic his brother's clumsy, loose-limbed way of moving; but there was nothing he could do to change his different-colored eyes to fit Noah's. Fortunately, Ma's eyesight was failing, and also after all these years, she'd gotten so used to seeing her sons together that she took their mirror images for granted.

Now, as they left the swamp and turned onto the service road leading toward Slidell, Nash looked back at his brother lying, drugged, on the narrow pull-down bed and hoped that Noah wouldn't wake up before they reached the hospital. Earlier, he'd asked his mother why they were taking 'Nash' to New Orleans and she had replied: 'Your brother, he goin' to have *une opération*.'

Nash frowned. Of all the reasons he'd considered, surgery hadn't been one of them. The idea enraged him. But he managed to stay calm. 'Why for he need that, Ma?'

'Is the Good Lord's wish, boy. He want Nash to be like you — gentle an' kind an' good to folks.'

'God told you that, Ma? Huh?'

'Sure did, son.'

At that moment Nash wanted to slit her throat and watch her gag on her own blood until her miserable life ebbed away. Instead, he said quietly: 'Nash ain't gonna like that, Ma.'

'It ain't up to him, son. Is God's wish. An' as His servants, is up to us to see the

Lord's wishes come true. You understand that, don't you, boy?'

'Sure,' Nash said. He turned to the window so she wouldn't see the rage in his eyes. 'I understand, Ma. I surely do. We doin' this to make God happy with Nash.'

'*C'est vrai*,' Ma said.

29

Cars and visitors came and went all morning. Occasionally an ambulance, siren wailing, pulled up to the emergency entrance. When the patient's condition was serious enough, it was met by a flurry of staffers, who tended to the patient even as the paramedics wheeled him or her inside the hospital.

Staked out in a quiet corner of the parking lot two CARD agents, one sitting behind the wheel of a First Communications telephone truck and the other, posing as a linesman halfway up a nearby pole, pretended not to be watching everything. Two more agents, parked in one of two black SUVs across the street from the main entrance, used pocket cams no bigger than matchboxes to tape everyone who entered or left. Agent Fuller surveyed the hospital and grounds from a vantage point above the Creole Dance Studio building a short distance to the south. And to the north and east, other rooftops were similarly occupied by the remaining two CARD agents.

In the main foyer Rosy and Hicks, posing as orderlies, kept watch on all the new arrivals. All the agents were in constant touch with Kate, who was running things from an empty third-floor office. Presently, her voice came through on their ear-mikes. 'Anything yet?'

''Nada,' Rosy said.

'All right, everyone. Keep alert. This could be a long day.'

Fuller's voice suddenly broke in: 'Wait a minute! I got something.'

'Talk to me,' Kate said.

From the dance studio roof, Agent Fuller followed her target through a pair of Bushnell PowerView binoculars. 'I got a Chevy camper,' she reported. 'Brown, model eighty-three, I think . . . local plates . . . heavyset gray-haired woman driving . . . can't make out the passenger, but it could be a guy.'

The camper drew level with the hospital entrance, its indicator-lights signaling a right turn. But at the last moment the camper drove on by, its turn-lights still blinking.

'Scratch that,' Fuller said. 'False alarm.'

Kate said: 'You sure? The suspect could be just circling, checking things out. I wasn't expecting a camper, but it fits the profile. Camper, pickup truck, SUV.'

'Forget it. She's driving away.'

'All right. Keep 'em peeled out there.'

Kate sensed someone behind her and turned to see Elliott entering. His haunted eyes asked the question that never left his mind. Kate shook her head: nothing so far.

'I thought she'd have been here by now,' he said.

'Kidnappers like to play mind games,' she explained. 'That way they make the victim more desperate to accept their terms.' She motioned to indicate someone was talking in her ear. 'Go ahead, Andrews.'

From his position halfway up the telephone pole, Tom Andrews, the CARD team agent posing as a linesman, said: 'Blue VW Westfalia camper. Nineteen-seventy, seventy-one. Driver a woman, fat, possibly mid-fifties. One male passenger, about thirty. Entering the lot now . . . pulling into a space . . . '

Kate said: 'Keep them in sight, but stay well back. Rosy? Make some noise.'

Rosy and Hicks moved to the glass entrance doors. Rosy said softly: 'We've got 'em, boss. They're getting another man out of the camper. He looks barely conscious.'

Kate said: 'As soon as they enter the hospital, bring them up here. Then I want you to run that license number through the local DMV. I want to know who owns that camper and where they live.'

'On it.'

Beside Kate, Elliott said: 'Is this it?'

'I think so,' she said.

30

Ten minutes later the elevator door
opened and Ma and Nash stepped out
onto the third floor opposite the nurse's
station. Hicks accompanied them, pushing the still-unconscious Noah in a
hospital wheelchair.

Kate, wearing a white doctor's coat,
calmly confronted Ma. 'I'm Dr Ward's
assistant. Is this the patient?'

'*Oui.*'

'He appears to be sedated.'

'I had to drug him,' Ma said, 'so's he
wouldn't cause no fuss.'

'I see.' Kate scribbled something on the
chart she was holding. 'What did you
use?'

'Laudanum.'

'You understand, I hope, that Dr Ward
won't be able to operate while he's in this
condition.'

Ma shrugged. 'We ain't goin' nowhere.'

'Good. We've prepared a room for him.

You can wait there while he's in pre-op.'

Ma balked and shook her head. 'No. I stay with my boy.'

'Ma'am, I'm not trying to be difficult. But you can't just walk in and have brain surgery. There are certain procedures that have to be followed. For obvious reasons we don't expect you to sign any consent forms, but we still have to check his blood type, his general fitness and allow the anesthesiologist to assess him — '

Ma eyed Kate flatly. 'I ain't arguin' that. But wherever my boy goes, *I* go. That's final.'

'Is there a problem here?'

Everyone turned as Elliott approached. He was desperately trying to hold himself together, but it was impossible to hide his loathing for this woman who'd abducted Chelsea.

'She says I can't go with my boy,' Ma said. She peered more closely at him. 'You're him, ain't you?'

'I'm Dr Ward, yes,' he replied stiffly. 'And you're the woman who's turned my daughter's life into a living hell. Is she all right?'

'*Oui* — s'long as you do like I say.'

'I've already agreed to that. Now, where is Chelsea? What have you done with her?'

Kate saw Elliott was close to losing it. 'Excuse me, Doctor,' she said, quietly but insistently.

He turned to her, calming. 'Yes? What is it?'

'I'm afraid there's going to be a slight delay. The patient has been given laudanum.'

Elliott turned to Ma. 'How much and how long ago?'

'Six drops. 'Bout two hours.'

Elliott leaned over Noah and gently peeled back his eyelids, noting without really thinking about it that he had *heterochromia*. He then took Noah's pulse and checked his heart with a stethoscope.

Ma said: 'He be all right, *oui?*'

'Yes.' Elliott turned to Hicks. 'Take them to the patient's room. I'll be along in a moment to administer a shot of Naloxone.'

'What's that?' Ma asked suspiciously.

'Something to bring him round enough

so I can operate on him,' Elliott said tersely.

He and Kate stepped back, allowing Hicks to wheel Noah down the hall. Ma and Nash, shuffling like Noah, followed them.

'Sorry,' Elliott said. ''Fraid I'm not handling this too well.'

'You're doing fine,' Kate assured him. She gazed after Ma. 'I wish I could read her mind. Doesn't she realize that by showing up here she's on the hook for kidnapping?'

'Maybe she thinks I'll drop the charges if I get Chelsea back. Either that or she doesn't care, just so long as her boy's okay.'

'Speaking of her boy, *is* he going to be okay?'

'I think so. But six drops — that's about fifty milligrams, give or take. She's lucky she didn't kill him.'

★ ★ ★

Kate and Elliott were in the empty third floor office, waiting for the Naxolone to take effect, when Kate's cell phone buzzed. 'I'm here, Rosy. What've you got?'

Rosy said: 'Name's Rebekah Fraya Guidry, nee Langlinais, address given as Middle Creek, St Tammany Parish. Separated, two sons, Nash and Noah, mirror twins. Noah's mentally impaired — '

' — which means we're dealing with Nash,' Kate said.

'Yeah, but get this. Her ex-husband was released from Elayn Hunt Correctional Facility about three days ago. Served fifteen years for armed robbery.'

'What's his name?'

'Peyton Guidry.'

'Good work, homey. Okay, I want a Hostage Rescue Team out to the Guidry place, *now*.' She turned to Elliott, adding: 'The net's tightening.'

'On them?' he asked bleakly. 'Or us?'

Ignoring his pessimism, she considered what Rosy had just told her. Unless she was mistaken, it seemed likely that Peyton Guidry's release from prison and Chelsea's abduction were related. But she knew better than to assume. Getting on the phone she got the number for Elayn Hunt and asked to speak with the

249

warden. When he came on the line, she explained who she was and said that she had reason to believe that a man released from his facility three days earlier might be involved in a crime she was presently investigating. 'His name is Peyton Guidry. I'd be grateful if you could pull the file on him and give me his complete record.'

'Be happy to,' the warden said. He brought Guidry's file up on his computer and read from it: 'He tried to rob a gas station in Slidell, approached a worker as she was taking trash to the garbage bin behind the building, pointed a .38 at her and told her to take him into the office out back. There he demanded that she open the safe. She resisted and during their scuffle, his gun went off. Guidry panicked and fled. Slidell police and St Tammany Parish sheriff's deputies were immediately alerted and he was picked up shortly thereafter.'

'What kind of a prisoner was he?'

'At first, hell on wheels. Had a hard-on for the world. But then we turned him. After that he basically kept to himself,

250

obeyed the rules, attended anger management classes and enrolled in our art class.'

'Were he and his wife close, do you know?'

'No. As soon as he was sentenced, she disowned him. Never came to his trial and we have no record of her ever visiting him or sending him mail.'

Kate frowned. That seemed to rule out any link between them. But remembering one of the rules of her training — *To understand the art, you must study the artist* — she asked as an afterthought: 'What kind of painting did Peyton pursue?'

'According to what it says here: Stylized Egyptian.'

Egypt again. 'Can you elaborate a little?' she asked.

'Well, apparently Guidry only painted three pictures and each was a portrait of a Pharaoh figure in profile, surrounded by hieroglyphs — same kind you see on the walls of tombs.'

'The hieroglyphs,' she said, 'does it say what they looked like?'

'No. But it does say that one of the paintings was a stylized self-portrait, with

Guidry wearing a crocodile headdress.'

'And the others?'

He read from his screen. 'Variations on the same theme. Anything else, Agent Palmer?'

'Thanks, no,' she said. 'You've been very helpful.' She ended the call, realizing that she had another connection to ancient Egypt. Also, a probable connection to Sobek. And another use of the number *three*.

Now if only she could figure out what it all meant.

31

The staff on the third floor had been instructed to stay away from Room 311. Hicks stood outside the door to make sure none of the staffers forgot and tried to enter.

Inside, Noah tossed and groaned in bed. Thinking he was Nash, Ma watched him with growing concern. Standing beside her, the real Nash was equally concerned. If Noah did or said anything to betray him, his act was over. Trying to hide his anxiety behind Noah's guileless façade, he watched his brother and thought, *Sleep, you dumb shit. Just sleep and don't give me away.*

In bed, Noah muttered incoherently: 'Pookie . . . want . . . P-Pookie . . . '

Ma frowned and turned to Nash. 'What for Nash want your turtle, son?'

Nash giggled, like Noah always giggled, and said: 'You ain't listenin' right, Ma. Nash, he ain't askin' for Pookie, he's sayin' he feels *poorly*.'

'You sure 'bout that?'

'Sure I'm sure.' He kept his head down, the bill of his cap hiding his eyes, so he couldn't see her expression and know if she believed him or not. Hoping to distract her, he asked: 'Is Nash gonna die, Ma? Did the coffee make him sick? Huh? Huh?'

Already on edge, Ma cuffed him. '*Bouche ta guile!*' she yelled. 'Go sit down!'

The blow wasn't hard, but it took Nash by surprise. He stumbled back into the bed tray, knocking over a plastic glass. It fell off the tray and instinctively he went to catch it with his left hand, the bell pinned to his denim coveralls tinkling. Almost in the same instant he realized his mistake and used his right instead. He deliberately fumbled the catch, knowing Noah couldn't catch anything, and the glass landed on the tile floor. Nash quickly retrieved it and set it on the tray.

'I'm s-sorry, Ma,' he stammered. 'W-Was a mistake. I didn't mean to knock it over. Honest.'

Before Ma could reply, the door

opened and Kate looked at them from the doorway.

'We're ready for your son,' she said.

★ ★ ★

One swing of his axe shattered the padlock. Peyton pulled open the door and stared, shocked, at the young girl crouching before him. Leaning his axe against the door jamb, he entered the woodshed and untied her gag.

'Who are you?' Peyton said. 'What're you doin' here?'

'M-my name's . . . Chelsea. P-Please don't hurt me.'

'Why would I want to hurt you, girl? Here, turn around so I can untie you.'

Chelsea obeyed and Peyton quickly freed her hands. Helping her up, he again asked her what she was doing there. Losing some of her fear of him, she explained about the kidnapping. He looked at her in astonished disbelief.

'It sounds crazy, I know,' Chelsea said. 'But it's true. I swear. I mean, why else would I be locked in here?'

There was logic to that. But still not convinced she was telling the truth, he said: 'Bekah — Ma — say why she kidnapped you?'

'No. But I bet it's got something to do with my Dad.'

'Why you think that?'

''Cause he's famous, and he's got a lot of money. 'Sides, she knew his name. When I opened my hotel door she asked me if 'Dr Ward' was there.'

Peyton eyed her suspiciously. 'You sayin' Ma kidnapped you so she could make your Daddy pay to get you back?'

Chelsea nodded.

'That don't make sense, girl. She's got a pile of faults, but greed ain't one of 'em. Long as I knowed her, she's never lusted after money.'

'Maybe she's changed,' said Chelsea. 'Or maybe there's another reason. I don't care. I just want to get away from here and back to my Dad.' Desperate, she added: 'If you help me, mister, I know he'll pay you a reward.'

Peyton wasn't listening. He was too busy remembering how Bekah had threatened to shoot him if he tried to see the boys. But was that her real reason? Or did the old sow not want him around because he might screw up her ransom plans?

This girl was worth money, maybe a lot of it. Money he could certainly use a share of. But more than that, she could be the very leverage he needed to force Bekah to let him see his boys.

'Are you listening to me?' Chelsea demanded. 'I said my Dad would pay you a reward if you'll take me back to him?'

Peyton's only response was to gag her again.

32

While the patient was in pre-op, Kate got a call on her cell. She answered immediately. Elliott watched her face, searching for a sign that would tell him Chelsea had been rescued and there'd be no need to go through with this fake operation.

But her expression remained blank. And after instructing the caller to keep the Guidry house staked out, she ended the call and told Rosy that the Hostage Rescue Team had come up empty.

'Damn.'

'So Chelsea wasn't there?' said Elliott.

'Nope.'

'They say anything else?'

Kate hesitated. 'They found a body in one of the upstairs rooms,' she said. To Rosy she added grimly: 'Deputy Doucet.'

'*What? Mi Dios!* How long has he been dead?'

'They estimate about eighteen hours.'

'Man, what a bummer.'

Elliott sagged. 'Then that confirms it.'

Kate nodded. 'You're about to operate on the Bayou Butcher. And there's something else,' she said to Rosy. 'The HRT found a chain and padlock in the same room as the body.'

He made the connection at once. 'Those traces we found at the Clemenceau place — steel alloy and zinc plating.'

'We won't know for sure until we make a match, but it sure looks like it.'

'So what about Chelsea?' Elliott demanded. 'Where's she being held? And who's got her? This Peyton character?'

'I don't know,' Kate said. 'But I promise you this, Elliott: sooner or later the Guidrys are going to lead us right to her.'

★ ★ ★

Everything about the operation was made to look as realistic as possible.

Elliott joined his staff gathered around the patient, and made a small incision just

259

above the patient's left ear. He implanted a miniature tracking device and then deftly sutured the wound.

What came next was purely for appearances' sake. He simply made a second small incision in the scalp over the patient's frontal bone, then closed it with sutures. The whole procedure was so easy that he could have almost performed it with his eyes shut. Yet he was sweating profusely when he finished, and his heart was racing.

'We'll need DNA and fingerprints when you're done,' Kate said when he wiped his forehead.

He nodded. 'No problem. This won't take long now.'

'Rosy, as soon as we get some prints, fax 'em through to the lab and tell them I want the results like, yesterday.'

'You'll get 'em, *jefe.*'

Elliott made a quick incision just below the patient's left collarbone and inserted the Implantable Pulse Generator. It was a remarkable device, thin, not much bigger than a silver dollar and less than an ounce in weight. He sutured the wound, then stood back to allow the rest of the team to finish off.

Removing his mask, he looked at Kate. 'Bastard's yours,' he said. 'I'm all done here.'

* * *

To allay any suspicions Ma might have, they waited another half-hour before wheeling the patient out of the O.R. Noah's head was swathed in bandages and a gauze pad had been taped over the site of the IPG implant. They wheeled him past Ma and Nash toward the recovery room.

Ma jumped up and started after them. Rosy quickly intercepted her. 'Sorry, ma'am. You'll have to wait here.'

Before she could argue, Kate and Elliott emerged from O.R.

'My boy,' Ma said to Elliott. 'How is he, *docteur?*'

'The surgery went well,' he said flatly. 'Soon as he's fully recovered, you can take him home.'

''Mean he don't have to stay here overnight?'

'No.'

'You're sure 'bout this?' She sounded wary.

He said sourly: 'I'm the man who invented the surgery, remember?'

'Did you do it, *docteur*? Did you cure my son?'

'Only time will tell that.'

'How much time?'

Elliott shrugged. 'You should see definite improvement in a few days. All right,' he added curtly, 'I've done what you wanted. Now I want my daughter back.'

'Soon as I get my boy home, I call you an' say where she is.'

'And I'm supposed to take your word for that?'

'I got no reason to hurt her. God showed me a way to save my son, an' I took it, same as any mother would.'

'We could arrest you right here and now, you know,' Kate reminded her.

'*C'est vrai.* But you won't. I be the only one knows where Dr Ward's daughter is. An' if I so much as smell the police on my tail, I will drive around till her guts rot.'

Seething, Elliott took a step toward Ma.

Kate quickly stepped between them and led Ma away. 'All right. We'll play this your way — ma'am. You can wait for your boy in Recovery.'

★ ★ ★

Though it galled Kate to let them go, she knew she had little choice. Besides, she was only releasing Ma temporarily. And when she finally cuffed the woman — and the Bayou Butcher — victory would taste all the sweeter.

But now, at the end of a long, hot, tense afternoon, that wasn't much consolation. And as she stood with Elliott in the hospital entrance, watching Ma, her son and Rosy wheeling the still-drowsy patient toward the old VW camper, she felt her frustration growing and sensed as much in Elliott.

Teeth gritted, he said: 'I can't believe we're letting that old bitch walk free.'

'Me either. But I've met her kind before. Tough as combat boots. She'd never crack under questioning. And without her, we might never find Chelsea.'

Having reached the camper, Ma opened the side door and then stood back as Rosy helped Nash get his brother into the vehicle and onto the pull-down bed. Ma then closed the door and glared at Rosy. 'Remember, *m'sieur* — no police.'

She opened her bag and allowed him to see the old .45 automatic there.

'Don't worry, ma'am,' he said softly. 'I got the message.'

33

Ma turned left onto Tulane Avenue and then took the right ramp for I-10, heading for Slidell, unaware that she was being tailed by two Chevy Suburbans containing Kate's team of Bayou Butcher and CARD agents.

Neither was she aware of the Astar AS350 B2 helicopter which took to the air less than five minutes after she'd left the hospital. From the skies above metropolitan New Orleans Kate, Elliott and Rosy were able to follow her every move, not just visually but via the chip implanted in Noah's head.

Squashed behind the wheel, Ma tried to concentrate on her driving, but it was almost impossible. All she could think about was that she'd done it! With God's help she'd actually pulled it off. She'd given Nash a second chance at life and given Noah a brother who'd look after him when she was dead.

For the first time in years, she felt almost content. And why not? *You should see definite improvement in a few days,* the doctor had told her. A few days! *Mon Dieu,* so soon!

In the back of the camper, sitting beside the unconscious Noah, Nash also had reason to celebrate. After all these years, he'd finally figured out a way to walk free for good. And in the end it had all been so easy.

New Orleans fell behind them. Through the smudgy window he saw the Mississippi Delta and wetlands stretching toward the northwest, its surface and black-earth levees speckled with ducks, coots and piping plovers, while sweeping masses of migrating snow geese circled overhead.

About thirty minutes later Ma took the right ramp for US-190 and Nash felt the camper slow down. He peered through the window, craning his neck to make sure the police hadn't set up any roadblocks ahead. In Noah's voice he called out: 'What is it, Ma? Why we stoppin'? Huh? Huh?'

'We not stoppin',' she replied. 'Gettin'

misty up ahead, is all. Got to slow down.'

Hearing their voices, Noah began to stir. Shortly he opened his eyes, saw his brother seated next to him, said weakly: 'W-Where am I, Nash? Wha' happened, huh?'

Nash looked long and hard at his mirror image. 'Shhhh,' he whispered. 'You're not supposed to talk. If Ma hears you, she'll get mad at you.'

For a moment it looked like Noah might cry.

'All right, all right,' Nash said quickly. 'I'll tell you. But then you got to go to sleep, okay?'

Noah nodded and beamed foolishly. 'I will, Nash. Honest to God.'

'You slipped and fell in the kitchen, whacked your head on the table and it wouldn't stop bleeding. So Ma an' me, we had to take you to *l'hôpital*. Now go to sleep.'

'But I been asleep,' Noah protested. 'For hours, seems like.' He suddenly noticed how Nash was dressed. 'Why for you got my clothes on? Huh? An' my cap?'

Before Nash could reply, Ma's voice bellowed through the plywood partition. 'How's he doin'?'

'Fine, Ma,' Nash said. 'He's doin' fine. Honest.'

Noah, hearing Nash mimicking his voice, started to say something. But Nash quickly clamped a hand over his mouth.

'Want me to sit up front with you, huh, Ma? Huh?'

'No,' she said. 'You stay there, boy. Look after your brother. Make sure Nash don't fall out of bed 'case I have to make any sudden stops.'

'Sure, Ma. I can do that.' Nash removed his hand from Noah's mouth and put a warning finger to his lips.

Confused, Noah said: 'Why for you talkin' like me, Nash?'

'Is a secret.'

'What kinda secret, huh? Huh?'

'I can't tell you.'

'Why not?'

''Cause I can't trust you. Last time you swore on the Bible, remember, and you still told Ma.'

Noah looked ashamed. 'I know, an' that

was bad of me. But I won't be bad again, I swear. Honest to God.' Tears glinted in his eyes. 'Please tell me the secret, Nash. Please.'

Nash sighed. 'Okay,' he said, resigned. 'But I warn you, Little Brother. Rat on me again and I'll never forgive you. Never, understand?'

'*Oui, oui.* I won't tell. Promise.'

'I'm pretending to be you.'

'Huh? Why for you doin' that?'

'To save you from a whippin'.'

'Huh?'

'If Ma had smelled coffee on your breath, she would've beat you till you couldn't walk.'

Noah had forgotten all about the coffee. Everything now made sense to him. 'An' she ain't catched on yet?'

'Nope. But the way she keep' looking at me, I think she's getting suspicious.'

Noah beamed. 'Well, you don't worry none 'bout me tellin' her, Nash, 'cause I never will. Never. Honest to God. 'Less of course I forget,' he added.

'Then you'd better not forget,' Nash warned.

'I won't. I won't forget, ever. Promise on the Bible.' He paused, worried, then said: 'But you won't get mad at me if I *do*, will you? If I forget an' tell Ma, I mean. You won't, will you, Nash? Huh? Huh?'

'No,' Nash said gently. 'I won't get mad.'

'Promise?'

'Promise.' He leaned over and kissed Noah on the forehead. 'How could I ever get mad at you? I love you, *mon p'tit frère*.'

* * *

Aboard the helicopter Kate said into her ear-mike: 'Ground units, drop back. The traffic's thinning out ahead and I don't want you spotted.'

'Affirmative,' Agent Fuller replied. Her phone vibrated. She answered it immediately, having to shout above the sound of the rotors. 'Palmer.'

'This is Les Fields, Agent Palmer. I've fast-tracked that fingerprint-identification you requested.'

'Great. There's a match, right?'

'Wrong.'

'*What?* There's got to be.'

'I ran it three times just to make sure, but there's no match. Whoever those prints belonged to hasn't been anywhere near the crime-scenes.'

Stunned, Kate ended the call. She'd been so *sure*. How could she have made such a mistake?

Seeing her disappointment, Rosy asked her what was wrong.

'Nash Guidry,' she said. 'He's not the Butcher.'

'You *serious?*'

'Yeah, there's no match.'

'Then who the fuck is he?'

'I don't know. All I know is we're back to square one.'

Wedged between them Elliot said: 'Is this going to affect finding Chelsea?'

''Course not,' Kate said. 'I promised you we'd find her and find her we will.'

★ ★ ★

As Ma's camper turned left onto Gause Boulevard, Nash looked out the window and saw they were heading into a thickening mist. They drove on, following the service road that led to Crawford's Landing. Shortly before they reached it, Ma turned onto a thin natural trail. Almost hidden by foliage and mist, it followed a green waterway back toward Middle Creek.

On the fold-down bed Noah said: 'My head hurts, Nash.'

'Keep your voice down, dummy!'

'But it hurts,' wailed Noah. 'Honest.'

When Noah started to cry Nash quickly unpinned the tiny bell pinned to his coveralls and gave it to him.

'Here — shut up and play with this.'

As Noah amused himself with the bell, Nash threw one more glance out the window and said softly: 'I guess it's time.'

Noah frowned. 'Time for what, Nash? Huh?'

'This,' said Nash.

He brought the cushion he'd been holding behind him around and pressed it firmly over Noah's face.

Noah instinctively struggled and tried to fight him off. But Nash leaned forward, over Noah, and used all his weight to keep his brother pinned down.

Noah's feet began to kick a panicky tattoo. Ma heard his feet drumming against the paneling and glanced over her shoulder. In doing so she lost her concentration and the camper swerved. Alarmed, she faced front again and in her haste over-corrected the wheel. The camper veered violently to the left, branches scraping along both its sides.

In back, the swerving dumped Nash and Noah off the bed. Noah, underneath his brother, cracked the left side of his head on floor.

Nash heaved him back onto the bed and once more stuffed the cushion down over his face. Noah's big, clumsy hands clawed at the air. Above the grind of the camper's engine Nash heard the pitiful squeals he made. He wondered if Noah thought he was playing, that he'd take the cushion away at the last moment and there'd be no harm done.

He hoped not.

Finally Noah's struggles began to subside. A short time later he lay absolutely still. Nash took the pillow from his face and tossed it aside.

Nash stared at his brother for several moments, then carefully positioned Noah's head on the pillow. It was then he realized Noah's eyes were staring at him. Worried that Ma, even with her failing eyesight, might notice Noah's blue and blue-gray eyes were the opposite of his, Nash gently closed his brother's eyelids. Then he turned and faced the partition separating him from his mother.

'Ma,' he screamed in Noah's voice. 'Ma, stop, quick! Hurry! Somethin's wrong with Nash! Honest!'

34

When Noah's head hit the camper floor, it damaged the IPG implanted just above his ear and the tracking signal went dead.

Kate reacted immediately. 'Pull over, everyone! Looks like we might have a glitch up here.'

The pilot brought the chopper to a hover. Below, their view of the swamp was hidden by a low-hanging mist. 'What's gone wrong?' she asked him.

The pilot shrugged. 'Could be the signal's been degraded by the fog or the humidity. Might even be that all the trees down there are interfering with reception.'

'Or maybe Ma's found the tracking device and removed it,' Elliott said gravely.

'I doubt that,' Kate said. Then: 'All right. We'll wait a while and see what happens. Everyone, hold your positions.'

* * *

Ma slid open the camper side-door and squeezed inside. The old VW rocked violently beneath her. Elbowing Nash aside, she leaned over Noah's body. 'W-What happened to him?'

'I dunno,' Nash said, pretending to be agitated. 'I dunno, I dunno, I dunno . . .'

'Calm down, son, calm down. I ain't sore at you. Try to think an' tell me exactly what happened.'

'Me'n Nash, we was just talkin' about Pookie, an' all of a sudden he give this big groan an' wouldn't talk no more.'

Ma cupped her fat-fingered hands about Noah's face and gently shook it. When there was no response, she bent to listen for his heartbeat.

'He ain't breathin'!' she exclaimed. Panicking, she slapped his face several times. Noah didn't respond, but as his body's muscular system relaxed after death, his eyelids slowly reopened. Unaware of it, Ma began alternating between pushing on Noah's chest and performing mouth-to-mouth resuscitation.

Nash shuffled nervously around, as he'd seen Noah do so often, and tugged impatiently on Ma's arm. 'What's wrong, Ma? What's wrong? Why ain't he breathin', huh? Huh?'

'Shut up!' she yelled, and went on trying to revive Noah. But still he failed to respond.

Finally, she leaned over the body, caressed Noah's cheek and started sobbing.

'Is he d-dead, Ma?' Nash asked, stammering like Noah. 'Is he? Is he? Huh? Huh?'

Ma sniffed back her tears and nodded.

Nash buried his face in his hands and wailed.

'That *bâtard!*' Ma hissed. 'He done this deliberate!'

'Who, Ma? Who?'

'Dr Ward! Said he could cure Nash, but all along he knowed what he was gonna do. He was gonna kill him!'

Nash wailed even harder.

Ma turned back to her dead son. 'I promise you, boy,' she said grimly. 'I take care of *le docteur.* He's now goin' to find out what it's like to lose *un enfant* of his own.'

She kissed Noah's pallid, bandaged forehead. Her tears spilled across his face and she gently wiped them away.

'Ahh, Nash,' she wept. 'I'm sorry, son . . . so sorry for what I done to you . . .' She leaned forward, intending to kiss him — and noticed something glinting among the folds of the blanket. Leaning closer, she picked it up and squinted at it.

It was the tiny chrome bell Leblanc had given Noah.

Puzzled, she showed it to Nash. 'Why for your brother got your bell, boy?'

For once Nash was caught off-guard. 'I don't know,' he said in his own voice. 'It must've come — ' Catching himself, he quickly became Noah again and pointing to the safety pin on his coveralls, stammered: ' . . . m-must've come loose. Yeah, yeah, that's it. It c-come loose when, y'know, you swerved an' I had to hold onto him so's he didn't f-fall out of bed. Honest, Ma. That's what happened . . .'

Suspicious, Ma glared at him for a moment. Then, sensing something was wrong, she turned back to Noah and peered closer at him.

It was then she saw his eyes were open.
She went to close the lids — and stopped.

Nash's eyes were gray-blue and blue.

The eyes of the corpse were blue and gray-blue.

This wasn't Nash staring blankly at her — it was Noah!

For several breathless moments she tried to make sense of her discovery. Then, numb with disbelief, she slowly turned back to Nash.

He started to say something inane, like Noah would have; but the look of hatred in Ma's eyes, the way her meaty fists were clenched, silenced him.

'You!' she hissed, shaking the bell at him. 'YOU!'

Just then Nash, too, saw that Noah's eyes were open.

He froze.

'Damn you, boy! I *knowed* there was somethin' wrong! Knowed it the minute you tried to catch that glass with your left hand in *l'hôpital!*'

She lunged for him. Nash angrily pushed her away, no longer pretending to be Noah. 'Get off me you big tub of pig fat!'

Ma came at him again, her face contorted with fury. 'You be the devil incarnate,' she raged. 'Your brother's dead on account of you!'

'Me? You're the one wanted the operation!'

'It was the Lord's will! His way of tamin' the devils trapped inside you . . . '

'If it was God's will, you righteous crow, then how come Noah died 'stead of me?'

Ma had no answer. She shook her head at Nash, unable to believe just how deep his evil ran. Simultaneously she realized that the only way to *really* cure him had been within her grasp all along.

Without warning she smashed him backward. The side-door of the camper was still open and unable to save himself he fell out and went sprawling to the ground. Spiked by adrenalin Ma charged after him. Nash scrambled out of her way. But Ma made no attempt to pursue him; instead she waddled to the driver's-side door and yanked it open.

'I'm goin' to hell on 'count of you,' she cursed. 'But I sure as sin ain't goin' alone!' Reaching into her bag, she started to take out the .45. 'As God is my witness, Nash Guidry, I'm takin' you with me!'

'Like hell you are!'

Nash pulled Doucet's Glock from his coveralls and as Ma began to swing the semi-automatic around he knocked the barrel aside, jammed the Glock deep into the folds of fat around her stomach and pulled the trigger, twice.

The shots sounded more like muffled pops.

Ma buckled and staggered back. Nash heard the air wheeze out of her. She stared at him, eyes bugged in shock, unable to believe what he'd done.

Nash smiled, enjoying himself as he watched her die at long last.

Ma tried to speak. Only blood came out. Then she collapsed at his feet, the front of her old wraparound dress stained red.

35

They sat waiting in the hovering helicopter for almost ten minutes. It was time Kate felt she really couldn't afford to lose, and when the tracking signal remained silent, she told her ground units that she was coming down to join them. 'We may have G.P.S. on our side,' she said to Rosy and Elliott, 'but we can't see much in this ground fog.'

★ ★ ★

Nash was sweating by the time he'd finished dragging Ma down to the water's edge. The mist was patchier here. He left her sprawled beside Noah, then quickly stripped to the waist.

From his pocket he took his latex gloves and gut-hook knife. Then he squatted beside Ma and set to work.

When he was finished, he used her blood to draw the three Egyptian symbols that spelled *SOBEK* across his torso. He then picked up Noah and carried him to a grove of live oaks growing a little farther along the riverbank.

There, he gently placed his twin between the gnarled roots of one of the trees. Sitting beside him, Nash stared out at the calm, mist-shrouded water. 'It's quiet now,' he told the corpse. 'No more whippings, no more hollerin' or arguin' at mealtimes. Just us, Noah, you and me, happy, just like when Pa used to take us fishin'.'

He paused as he heard vehicles approaching in the distance and looked off between the oak trees to the road, but saw only patches of lazy mist. Still, the sound of engines made him uneasy. He reminded himself again that there was always the chance that they'd been followed from New Orleans.

He leaned over and kissed Noah's cheek. '*Sommeil bien, mon p'tit frère.*'

He was returning to the camper to collect his discarded shirt and John Deere cap when two black SUVs drove cautiously around a bend in the trail about a hundred yards away. Nash glimpsed their headlights shining dully through the haze. He grabbed his Glock, knife and a small bundle he'd fashioned from a grubby handkerchief, and ran back into the trees.

There, he held his breath. If the vehicles drove past, then all was well. If they stopped, it probably meant they were occupied by the sheriff or some type of federal lawmen.

A few moments later the SUVs pulled up behind the camper, and Nash fled.

* * *

The pilot finally managed to find an opening in the mist. Descending, the chopper's rotors ruffling the treetops and the surface of the water, he set Kate, Elliott and Rosy down on a patch of mossy ground beside the trail, close to the parked SUVs. He then took off again, with orders to fly above the low-hanging mist but to stay close.

Ducking out from under the chopper's noisy downdraft, the three of them hurried to the blinking hazard lights of the lead SUV. Agent Fuller sat at the wheel. Hicks, who'd been riding shotgun, got out so Kate could sit up front. He then climbed in back with Rosy and Elliott. She checked the monitor again, but the signal still hadn't come back.

'What the hell are they doing?' muttered Elliott.

'I don't know,' Kate said. 'But I think we've waited long enough to find out.'

She gave the order to move in and Fuller edged the Suburban forward through the mist with the second SUV, containing the CARD team, creeping along behind them.

Five minutes later they came out of the trees. Here, sunlight had burned off most of the mist and almost immediately they saw Ma's camper parked up ahead, its side door open.

Elliott thought painfully, *Chelsea* . . .

As they drew closer it became obvious that the camper had been abandoned. The SUVs pulled up behind it and everyone spilled out.

'They must be somewhere close,' Kate said, checking the monitor.

'I got blood here,' a CARD agent named Barry Teague called urgently. 'And a shirt and cap.'

Kate, Rosy and Elliott hurried around the camper. The driver's-side door was ajar, and an old .45 semi-automatic lay on the ground. Blood sparkled dark and wet in the flattened grass, marking a trail down toward the water. Farther along the bank lay a discarded shirt and a John Deere cap.

Kate turned to Elliott. 'Maybe you shouldn't see this.'

'Try and stop me,' he said.

They watched as Rosy followed the blood-trail down to the water and then waded through the tall reeds until he found what he was looking for. He paused to quickly examine the corpse before turning to Kate. 'It's the Guidry woman,' he said. 'What's left of her.'

'Keep looking,' she said grimly.

'Looks like that's it,' called Rosy.

'Okay, so what the fuck do we do now?' Elliott asked Kate. 'The Guidry woman said she was the only one who knew where Chelsea is!'

Needing time to think, Kate turned to two of the CARD agents, Andrews and Larkin. 'Help Rosy bring the body ashore and then notify Slidell PD and the New Orleans field office.'

Elliott grasped her arm. 'Kate?'

She was about to tell him to keep calm, that this wasn't over yet, when she spotted what appeared to be a man propped against a tree a short distance away. Pushing past Elliott, she ran toward him.

As she got closer she saw it was the suspect they'd identified as Nash Guidry. She knelt beside him and checked for a pulse, sensing even as she did so that he was dead.

Elliott came up behind her.

She examined the corpse, but could find no obvious cause of death. So what had happened to him? An adverse reaction to the anesthetic, perhaps, or the laudanum his mother had first used to drug him?

'He's suffered some kind of trauma to the head,' said Elliott, kneeling to make a quick examination of his own. 'That's

287

why we lost the goddamn signal.'

Kate looked back at the camper. Rosy, Andrews and Larkin were dragging the Guidry woman's body ashore.

If Nash was dead, then who had killed his mother?

The idiot son in the John Deere cap?

The same cap that now lay atop the neatly-folded shirt?

That just didn't make sense.

Unless . . .

She studied the face of the dead man, trying to read from his slack expression just how this situation had come about. But the corpse wasn't revealing anything.

Then she became very still, thinking: *The hell it isn't.*

She leaned close and looked at the face. The eyes were dull, almost obscured by the half-closed lids. But for the first time she realized that the eyes were different colors.

'Take a look at his eyes, Elliott.'

'He's got *heterochromia*, sure,' he replied. 'I noticed it when I first examined him.'

'And in his mirror twin?'

'It would be reversed.'

Reversed? Kate thought.

Oh Christ —

She took out her cell and speed-dialed. A moment later she said: 'Les?' The reception was terrible. 'This is Agent Palmer. Listen — I want you to check those fingerprints for me again, but this time I want you to flip them . . . No not *skip* them, *flip* them — F-L-I-P. That's right, so that they're mirror images. Then get back to me ASAP, okay?'

As she ended the call Elliott said: 'Jesus, are you saying I operated on the wrong son? That I should have operated on the retard?'

'This *is* the retard,' she said grimly. 'I don't know how he talked his brother into it, but somehow Nash switched places with Noah without their mother knowing — and he's still out there, somewhere.'

Elliott paled. 'And so is Chelsea,' he said.

★   ★   ★

Nash splashed joyously through the misty woods. He leapt over deadfalls and weaved between vine-draped trees, sweat running down his blood-streaked torso.

Never in his wildest fantasies had he realized that freedom could feel this exhilarating. No more chains, no more chalk lines, no more whippings. The remainder of his life lay before him, just waiting to be taken and lived, and he was going to live it to the full.

Hell, he was going to live it to the *hilt*.

The dense woods edging the swamp became more and more familiar. As he got closer to home and the date he'd promised himself with the girl Ma had locked in the woodshed, he paused to catch his breath.

Tired but exhilarated, he leaned back against an old cypress tree and filled his lungs with cool, damp air. Delusions of grandeur swept through his twisted mind. He felt almost drunk with power . . . with the knowledge that from now on the swamp and surrounding bayous were like a human smorgasbord that was his for the taking. He would terrorize them while at the same time appease Sobek . . . and because he was all-powerful he would remain at large forever . . .

Suddenly he stiffened.

Off to the north he heard vehicles approaching. Since there were no other roads in this remote area, they could only be heading for the house. He guessed it was the law . . . a posse looking for Deputy Doucet's body . . . or maybe him . . . or even the girl. He gritted his teeth, disappointed that she would be rescued before he could get his hands on her.

Still, there'd be other young girls . . . lots of them.

But the presence of the law also meant the house was now out of bounds. He'd planned to return there, have his fun with the girl, then take what he needed in the way of clothes, supplies and Ma's meager savings, and disappear into the swamp.

Having the law breathing down his neck changed all that. Now he had to get out and away before they caught him. But where else could he hole up temporarily? He was near-naked and penniless. He could go nowhere until he had money and clothing.

He needed a place to hide until he worked out his next move . . . and even as he thought it, so the answer came to him.

Rising, he hurried off in another direction.

36

The two mud-spattered SUVs followed the narrow winding trail as it skirted the western edge of the swamp.

In the lead vehicle Kate said: 'He can't have gotten far.'

'Yeah, but where's he headed?' said Rosy. 'For all we know he had a boat stashed somewhere and right now is paddling into the swamp.'

'If it were me, I'd head home,' Agent Fuller said. She was driving as fast as she dared, alternately braking and accelerating as the ever-narrowing trail snaked between the trees and dense, waterlogged undergrowth. 'I mean, he's on the run and probably needs to pick up some things before he goes to ground.'

'We should be so lucky,' Kate said. ''Cause then he'll walk right into the arms of the Hostage Rescue guys.'

'You're forgetting Chelsea,' Elliott said. 'Before the bastard killed his mother I bet he forced her to tell him where my daughter's hidden. *That's* where he's headed.'

Kate knew he could be right, but not wanting to confirm his fears she kept silent. Ahead the trail curved past a small, wood-framed general store with a rusty *Drink Jax Beer* sign above the door. 'Pull over,' she told Fuller.

Inside, the dimly-lit store smelled of praline and mayonnaise, sawdust and sauces. Flies buzzed against a rear window that overlooked the swamp. Jean Leblanc stood halfway down the first aisle, dusting the oil lamps and tubular lanterns on the top shelf. He looked around as they crowded inside and recognizing Rosy, politely nodded.

'FBI,' Kate said, showing her ID.

'My daughter's been kidnapped,' Elliott blurted, 'by a woman who lived around here, name of Guidry.'

Leblanc frowned. 'You make it sound like she ain't with us no more.'

'She's not. And neither's her son, Noah.'

The news rocked the old man. '*Mon*

Dieu,' he said softly. 'Does Deputy Doucet know this?'

'Did you know the Deputy?' Kate asked.

'*Mais oui*. We are old friends.'

'Then I'm sorry, *m'sieur*. Deputy Doucet's dead as well.'

'Murdered,' Rosy added, 'which is one of the reasons why we're here.'

Leblanc paled, badly shaken, and leaned against the shelf to steady himself. 'Who would do this awful thing?'

'That's what we're trying to find out,' Kate said. 'So if you know anything, anything at all that might lead us to the killer, please . . . tell me.'

Leblanc looked at Rosy. 'When you were in here before, *m'sieur*, asking 'bout latex gloves — did that have somethin' to do with Doucet's murder?'

'Probably, yeah,' Rosy said. 'But before we can prove it, we need to talk to Nash Guidry.'

'Nash at *la université*.'

'No, that was a lie,' put in Kate. 'Something his mother invented to protect him. We're pretty sure he's been hiding around here all the time.'

'Does he have any friends or relatives who might hide him?' Elliott asked.

'No, *m'sieur*. The Guidrys, they got no relatives. An' now that the Gaspards are dead, no real friends.'

'How about a favorite hideout?' said Rosy. 'Somewhere Nash and Noah might've hung out as kids?'

Leblanc shrugged. 'You might try Peetre's Pond. The boys, they used to fish there all the time when they was young. Their Pa, afore he went to prison, built 'em *une grand maison d'arbre*. It still be there, last I heard.'

Elliott turned to Kate. 'A tree-house? That'd be a great place to hide Chelsea.'

'How do we get there?' she asked Leblanc.

'Is no more'n two miles northeast, *madame*.' He indicated the lingering mist beyond the windows. 'But is not so easy to find, 'specially in *le brouillard* an' all.'

'Would you be willing to show us?'

Leblanc nodded. '*Pour le Depute Doucet, avec plaisir!*'

Outside, the rest of the team were gathered by the SUVs. Leblanc explained that they couldn't get to Peetre's Pond by vehicle, only by boat. He then led them alongside the store and down a grassy slope that ended at the water's edge. There sat a long, tarpaulin-covered boat. Leblanc pulled the tarp back to reveal a sixteen-foot, four-rib fiberglass pirogue with a flat stern and end compartments. Two paddles and a detachable trolling motor lay in the bottom.

'Help me get this in the water,' he said, 'an' then I take you where you want to go.'

'We can't all fit in it,' Kate said.

'*Bien sûr que non*. She will carry three, *et moi*. Your friends will have to stay behind, or find another boat.'

Kate signaled to Rosy and Hicks. 'You guys help him. Elliott, you stay here — '

'The hell with that! That's my daughter out there — '

She hesitated. He had a point, and she didn't have the time to argue it. 'All right,' she said. 'Hicks, you stay behind with the others. Everyone spread out and beg, borrow or steal whatever boats you can, but get to that tree-house *ASAP*.'

37

It seemed like ages since Nash had last visited Peetre's Pond, but little had changed from his boyhood. Ahead stood the old twisted cypress, its gnarly roots buried half in the water, half in the bank. Through the drifting mist he could see the tree-house perched among the branches. In sorry condition, its walls and roof were overgrown by Spanish moss, white tree orchids and Virginia creepers.

Skirting the pond, he began to scale the frayed rope ladder dangling from the porch. He'd almost made it to the top when he heard a sound from within. He hung there, motionless, worried that the law had staked this place out, too. But then the sound came again and he realized it was a sob.

Cautiously he climbed onto the porch and pushed the door open. The first things he saw were three paintings tacked to the facing wall. Surprised, he studied them. They all showed a pharaoh-figure in profile, looking off to his left, wearing a headdress shaped like a crocodile head. He was surrounded by various symbols, three of which spelled SOBEK and were as familiar to Nash as his own signature. But it was the profile in the middle painting that fascinated him most of all.

It depicted a pharaoh who looked too much like his Pa to be mere coincidence. He stared fixedly at the rendering, the single visible deep-set blue eye, the shape of the mouth, the thrust of the jaw, and felt almost lightheaded.

It *was* Pa! And on either side of the other paintings was another profile . . . actually *two* profiles, when you looked closely and saw that one had a blue eye, the other blue-gray.

They were meant to be him and Noah.

Excited, he wondered who had left the paintings here. Had Noah been right when he said that Pa was getting out of prison? He had to be. There was no other answer.

Something stirred to his right. Nash whirled and aimed his gun at it. That's when he saw her and his world began to spin. He sank to his knees, a look of beatific gratitude on his face, and stuffed the gun into his pants. If he had wanted any further proof that he was carrying out the work of some higher power, he need look no farther than this.

For the girl hadn't been taken from him after all. She'd merely been transferred from the woodshed to *here.*

Rising, he entered the tree-house, the floor swaying underfoot, and approached Chelsea. She lay on a pile of dirty blankets. She was scratched and bruised and her clothes were stained with mud. Her hands and feet were tied and she was gagged. The fear he saw in her eyes made his blood sing.

He knelt before her. Frightened, she tried to squirm away from the half-naked, bloodstained apparition he had become.

'You don't have to be afraid no more,' he said gently. 'Ma's dead now. Noah, too.'

Chelsea said something that was muffled by the gag.

'If I untie that,' Nash said, 'you promise not to holler?'

When she nodded, he removed the gag and tossed it aside.

'P-Please,' she begged. 'Please let me go.'

'How did you get here?' he asked.

'A m-man. A man brought me.'

'What man?'

'I don't know. Tall, skinny . . . a long gray overcoat.'

Nash grasped her by the arms and shook her. 'What's his name?' he demanded.

'I don't know.'

'Don't lie to me! Who is he?'

She pointed at the middle painting. 'Him.'

So it was *Pa!* Elated, he said: 'Where is he now?'

'I d-don't know. He left. Hours ago. Can I go home now?' she begged.

'*Oui.* But first I show you my surprise.'

He took out a folding knife and opened the blade. Chelsea saw bloodstains on it and panicked. Nash pressed her against his bare chest. Then with one hand he cut the ropes binding her hands and ankles and helped her up.

'I-I don't want a surprise,' she said, scared. 'Please, I just want to go home.'

'*After* you've seen my surprise,' he insisted. 'Now, close your eyes.'

'Why?'

'Don't argue, just do like I say and nothin' bad will happen.'

Chelsea reluctantly obeyed.

She heard him move. She desperately wanted to open her eyes but was too afraid. Finally, she heard him say: 'All right, you can open them now.'

She obeyed.

His hand was held out to her, palm up. On it was a bloodstained handkerchief on which lay Ma's torn-out tongue and severed ears.

★　★　★

Propelled by Leblanc's old 24-volt trolling motor, the pirogue chugged through the seemingly endless swamp, following a maze of narrow, connecting waterways.

Frustrated by the slow pace, Elliott was barely able to contain his impatience.

302

Watching him, Kate knew he was going through ten kinds of hell and wished there was something she could do to ease his pain. As if answering her wish, her cell phone vibrated. Snatching it from her pocket, she checked the caller ID and said: 'Talk to me, Les.'

From his lab in Slidell, Les Field said: 'I flipped the suspect's prints, like you said.'

'And?'

'Don't ask me how, Kate, but you called it: they match.'

'Say again, Les. You're breaking up.'

'I said you got your match,' he repeated.

'Thanks. I owe you one.' As she tucked the phone away, she saw Elliott and Rosy watching her expectantly. 'We were right before,' she told them. 'Nash — the *real* Nash, that is — *is* the Butcher.'

Before they could react, the engine stopped. Surprised, they looked back at Leblanc and saw him swing the outboard motor over the stern so its propeller was out of the water.

'What's wrong?' Kate asked.

'Nothin', *madame*. This be as far as we can go.'

'*What?*'

They were still in the swamp, mist swirling around them.

'Everyone out, *s'il vous plait*,' Leblanc said. He stepped out of the boat, into water that barely reached over his ankles.

Kate, Elliott and Rosy quickly joined him. Pulling the boat behind him, Leblanc waded ahead of them. 'The channel, she narrow down to a slough up ahead,' he explained. 'Then she open out again into Peetre's Pond.'

'How far?' asked Kate.

'Forty, fifty yards, maybe less.'

'Good enough,' she said. 'You stay here, *m'sieur*. And thanks for all your —'

From somewhere ahead there came a scream.

A young girl's scream.

Elliott lost it. And before Kate could stop him, he yelled, '*Chelsea!*' and ran splashing past her into the undergrowth ahead.

★ ★ ★

304

Elliott elbowed his way through the tangled vines and bushes and stumbled into the clearing. Facing him was a small scummy pond. On the far bank, among the branches of an old cypress, was the tree-house Leblanc had told them about.

It looked abandoned.

Still not thinking straight, he yelled: 'Chelsea! Chelsea, can you hear — ?'

Just then Rosy tackled him from behind. Both went sprawling in the swamp grass. Before Elliott could say anything, Rosy clamped his hand over the neurosurgeon's mouth.

'Caution's the way,' he whispered. Then, removing his hand: 'Or next time, *amigo*, you might walk straight into a *bullet*.'

Realizing he was right, Elliott nodded his thanks.

Kate wriggled up beside them. 'See anything?' she asked Rosy, who was now scoping things out through mini-field glasses.

'*Nada*.'

'Now what?' Elliott asked Kate.

'We negotiate.' Rising onto her elbows

so she could see above the grass, she shouted: 'Nash Guidry? This is Agent Palmer, FBI. Can you hear me?'

No reply came from the tree-house.

'Nash! Listen to me! There's nowhere to run! I've got agents everywhere! You're surrounded!'

More silence.

'I want to help you! Do you understand?'

The silence persisted.

'Rosy,' Kate whispered.

He nodded, reading her mind. 'I'm on it, boss.' Then, to Elliott: 'Stay put, Doc.'

He crawled away.

Elliott soon lost sight of him, but followed his progress by watching the swaying of the tall grass. Rosy made his way around the pond, moving with infinite care and making use of every scrap of cover.

Kate cautiously got to her feet. Raising both hands, she called out to Nash. 'Let's at least talk about this. Okay?'

The tree-house remained as silent as a photograph.

Kate took a step forward, hands still

raised, ready to dive aside if Nash started shooting.

When he didn't, she took another step and then another. 'It's all right, Nash,' she called. 'Your mother can't hurt you anymore and neither can Noah! You're free of them now.'

Peripherally, she saw that Rosy was now crawling through the brush on the far side of the pond. He was close to the tree-house and to keep Nash occupied, she said: 'Talk to me, Nash! I'm curious. I want to know more about you . . . you and . . . Sobek.'

It was the hook with which she hoped to grab his attention; the one subject he might be willing to discuss.

But still there was no response.

Kate got a bad feeling. 'Nash? I know you can hear me. Why don't you tell me about Sobek?'

Sharing her misgivings, Rosy came out of the brush almost under the tree-house and peered up at the floorboards. There were cracks between the boards but nothing seemed to be moving inside. Puzzled, he glanced around and saw something hanging behind the tree. He ran to it.

Kate and Elliott waited anxiously.

A moment later Rosy reappeared. 'There's a back way out,' he told Kate. 'A missing panel and a length of rope. They've split.'

'Shit!'

He scrambled up the ladder. Reaching the porch he opened the door, looked inside. 'Better take a look at this, boss.'

Kate ran to the ladder, Elliott following. He waited for her to climb onto the porch and then hurried up after her.

'What do you make of these?' Rosy said as first Kate, then Elliott joined him in the tree-house.

Kate scanned the paintings. 'These must be ones Peyton Guidry did while he was in prison. See the resemblances,' she pointed, 'Nash, Peyton, Noah. Guess there isn't much doubt now that the father's involved in this somehow.'

'D'you think he's got Chelsea with him?' Elliott said.

Rosy shrugged and looked at Kate. 'We've got two cut lengths of rope, a rag that could've been used as a gag and a bloodstain — but nothing to prove that Chelsea was here.'

'Dammit,' Elliott said. 'I heard her scream.'

'You heard *a* scream,' Kate corrected. 'I admit it sounded like a girl, so it probably was her, but I'm assuming nothing.'

Rosy, who'd been examining some old blankets in the corner, said: 'They're still warm.'

Elliott sagged. 'Oh God, we were so close.'

'You recognize this?' Rosy asked him. He held out a small leather friendship bracelet he'd found on the blankets. The initials *CW* had been burned into it.

Elliott choked up. 'It's hers. I bought it for her in New Orleans. It must've come loose.'

'Don't underestimate her,' Kate said. 'Could be she left it there *deliberately*.'

When they were back on the ground Kate told Rosy to instruct the chopper pilot to make an aerial search of the area. As he got on his cell, she pulled out a Nextel PTT phone and thumbed *Direct*

Connect. 'All units,' she said, holding the phone like a walkie-talkie. 'This is Palmer. We're at Peetre's Pond. The perp has just taken off with the hostage, headed north. Remember, he's armed, and if he doubles back he'll be coming your way. Proceed with caution. Got that?'

She waited, but there was no response. 'Fuller? Hicks? Anyone? Answer me, dammit!'

Abruptly the phone squawked, and a voice that could have been Hicks, said: ' . . . you k . . . up . . . and . . . '

Kate said, 'Fucking reception,' and turned to Elliott. 'Looks like we're on our own. We'll spread out, but stay in sight. We're looking for tracks, signs, anything to tell us which way they went.'

When Rosy rejoined them, they fanned out and began splashing through ankle-deep loamy soil. They moved slowly, slower than Elliott liked, looking about them for possible clues.

Soon they were fifty yards apart but still moving in the same direction. A noise in the brush froze Elliott. He stood there, listening, ankle-deep in stagnant water.

Then he heard it again — a rustling in the bushes ahead.

Barely breathing, he stared at the brush. He thought of trying to attract Kate's attention, but didn't want to alert whoever might be hiding there. Instead, remembering Rosy's advice, he cautiously approached the bushes.

As he got close, the tangled brush exploded outward and a huge, wild boar burst from cover. On seeing him it lowered its bristly head and charged. Elliott dived aside, narrowly avoiding its gleaming tusks. The boar ran off, snorting, and disappeared into the trees.

Heart thudding, Elliott got up and wiped the mud from his face and clothes. He realized he was shaking. *Get a grip*, he told himself. *Focus. Chelsea's life is at stake.*

Calming, he started walking again. He'd only taken a few steps when he recognized an especially gnarly cypress. Realizing he'd gotten turned around and was headed in the wrong direction, he stopped and looked about for Kate and Rosy, but they were no longer in sight. He was lost.

38

Peyton Guidry knew something was wrong when he heard a helicopter circling overhead. He pushed on through the trees and soon came within sight of the house. He looked up. Through the canopy he spotted the unmarked chopper hovering below the clouds. Suspicious, he turned back to the house and this time noticed two combat rubber raiding craft moored beside a white skiff at the dock. Ducking behind a tree, he studied the house more carefully.

Earlier, he'd left the girl tied up in the tree-house and then headed here. He planned to wait until Bekah and the boys returned home. He'd then have his reunion with Nash and Noah and Bekah would just have to accept him because he, *Peyton*, had her hostage and was now calling the shots —

His thinking was interrupted as a man appeared around the side of the house.

He wore body armor over olive-green fatigues, carried a submachine gun and had goggles pushed back on his steel helmet. Peyton watched as the man climbed onto the porch, revealing the letters FBI printed across the back of his vest. Alarmed, Peyton realized that whatever Bekah was planning had been discovered by the Feds, who were now waiting for her and the boys to return so they could arrest them.

His first thought was for his sons. He didn't want them to go to prison and suffer as he had. But then he realized that when the Feds found the girl, she'd implicate *him*, too. Just days out of fucking prison and already involved in the kidnapping of a minor! He shook his head in disbelief. How much crap luck could any one man have?

Knowing the only way he could help his boys — and himself — was by staying out of prison, he hurried back toward Peetre's Pond. If he could get to the tree-house before the Feds and convince the girl that he'd actually *rescued* her and was now willing to take her back to her father, maybe her folks would be grateful enough not to press charges. It was a long shot, but the only option he could think of.

Throwing his overcoat over his shoulder, he took a short cut that forced him to wade through murky, thigh-deep water. Roots and weeds snagged his ankles, slowing him down, but he gamely struggled on and in twenty minutes or so was within a half-mile of the tree-house.

That's when he heard voices ahead. He stopped, alarmed, as he recognized one of them. It was the girl's. He was too late, then — she'd already been rescued!

Dejected, he continued on. He hadn't gone far when through the misty trees and foliage he glimpsed two figures just ahead of him. They were coming his way. Ducking behind a large vine-clad tupelo tree, he submerged himself up to his neck. As he peered between the twisted roots, he recognized the girl's yellow hair and knew he hadn't been mistaken, as he'd hoped.

But he was mistaken about something else: it wasn't the Feds who'd rescued her, but a tall, half-naked man whose chest was smeared with red symbols. His face looked familiar. Curious, Peyton watched him dragging the girl along and realized he'd made another mistake: the young man hadn't rescued the girl; she was his *prisoner*.

Peyton knew then that he'd been given another chance. Rescue the girl now and she'd be forever grateful. In the distance he heard the helicopter again. The Feds were coming! Time was running out. He tensed, ready to attack the man after he'd waded past him. But as he got closer, Peyton recognized him and his heart wedged in his throat: it was his boy, his favorite son —

It was *Nash*.

39

Kate turned to her left to see how Elliott was holding up. She couldn't see him. Even as she wondered where he was, the voice of the helicopter pilot came over her ear-mike.

'I've just spotted them,' he said. 'A young girl with blondish hair, being dragged along by a male . . . naked to the waist . . . some kind of writing on his chest . . . '

'That's our suspect,' Kate said. 'Where are they?'

'About three hundred yards north of your position.'

'Got it. Keep them in sight.'

She turned as Rosy, who was on the same frequency, came splashing up. 'Where's the Doc?' he asked.

'Over there in those trees somewhere,' she pointed.

'Want me to round him up?'

Kate locked gazes with him. They both knew what she was thinking: Elliott had proved earlier that he was a liability; one they didn't need while trying to rescue a terrified teenager from a killer.

'After we've got Chelsea back,' Kate said.

Guns drawn, they headed north.

★ ★ ★

Nash reared back as a figure suddenly rose out of water in front of him.

Beside him Chelsea screamed and tried to run. Nash jerked her back, pulling her off her feet so that she fell, face-down, in the water. He then pulled out his gun, ready to shoot — only to have the figure, a tall gaunt man in a shirt and jeans, with a Confederate overcoat draped over his shoulders, raise his hands and say: 'Don't shoot, son. It's me — your Pa.'

Nash peered in disbelief at the bedraggled figure, so skinny and haggard now, and realized that despite how much fifteen years in prison had aged him, it was indeed his father.

'Pa . . . ' he began.

At that moment Chelsea, on her feet now and dripping wet, held her hand out pleadingly to Peyton. 'H-Help me,' she begged. 'Please, mister . . . he's going to *kill* me.'

'Shut up,' Nash told her. Then: 'Don't listen to her, Pa. She — ' He broke off and looked up as the helicopter flew over, low enough to batter the canopy.

'Son,' Peyton said, 'let her go. Now. 'Fore the Feds find you.'

'No!'

'Be reasonable, boy. You don't, an' they'll throw the book at you — all three of you.' He waded forward, intending to help Chelsea, only to be pushed back by Nash.

'No,' he yelled. 'Get away! She belongs to Sobek.'

'Don't talk crazy, boy.' Peyton's voice was almost drowned out by the hovering chopper. 'You gotta get out of here, fast.' He turned to Chelsea, adding: 'If I help you get back to your Pa, girlie, you gotta promise me that you won't blame my boy, Nash, here — him, or his brother Noah, or their ma for puttin' the snatch on you — '

'You don't have to worry about them,' Nash told him. 'They're dead.'

He swayed. 'Dead? When? *How?*'

'*He killed them!*' screamed Chelsea. Then, as Peyton looked at her in disbelief: 'Look in his pocket! He's got his mom's ears and tongue wrapped in a handker-chief!'

Shocked, Peyton stared at Nash. 'That true, boy?'

His world died when Nash nodded.

'For the love of God, son, why for you do that?'

'For *you*, Pa. I did it for you. Sobek told me what I had to do to get you back an' I done it. And it worked. You're back again. With me.'

Peyton saw the madness in Nash's eyes, heard the fervor in his voice, and knew he had to get the girl away from him.

Unable to find words to express how he felt, he said numbly: 'That was wrong of you, boy. It's a mortal sin to take a life.'

'No, no, Sobek *told* me to do it and I done it and now it's just us, you 'n' me, Pa, together again like before.'

Overhead, the chopper dropped lower,

319

its downdraft flattening the canopy and ripping leaves from the branches.

Peyton knew then what he had to do. 'Son,' he shouted. 'We ain't got time to talk 'bout this now. Give me your gun an' I'll lead 'em away from you, *oui?*' He stretched out his hand but Nash stepped back, out of reach, and gripped Chelsea's arm so hard she whimpered.

'Please,' she begged Peyton. 'Don't leave me here with him! He's going to kill me!'

Nash slapped her. 'Come with me, Pa. We'll hide deep in the swamp, where they'll never find us.'

'Sure, son, sure. We can do that. But first I gotta lead 'em away so you can go back to the tree-house.' Before Nash could argue, Peyton threw his overcoat over a limb, stripped off his shirt and dived under the water. He surfaced about twenty feet away and looked back at Nash. 'I'll meet you there later. Then we be together again.' He swam off.

Nash stared after him for a moment, wondering why his Pa hadn't applauded what he was doing. Surely he, of all people, understood that Sobek's instructions had to be obeyed. Confused and disappointed, he turned back to Chelsea.

'P-Please,' she pleaded. 'Do as your Dad says. Let me go. I promise I won't tell them it was you. I'll say it was all your Mom's idea and — and then you won't get into trouble — '

Ignoring her, Nash grabbed his father's coat and dragged her off in another direction.

Overhead, the helicopter angled away, looking for another break in the treetops.

40

Kate and Rosy stopped, knee-deep in swamp water, as their ear-mikes came to life. It was the chopper pilot, confirming he was still in pursuit of the suspect, but that he was now alone.

'Where's the girl?' Kate said, heart sinking.

'I don't know. Could be he's ditched her to make better time.'

Or maybe he's killed her, thought Kate. She said: 'All right, Jeff. Stay with him. We're on our way.'

⋆ ⋆ ⋆

Elliott plodded wearily through the swamp. He still couldn't see Kate or Rosy and had no idea where he was going, but could only hope he was headed in the right direction. He was hot, frantic and nearing exhaustion, and only his love for his daughter kept him going.

Presently, a short distance ahead, he

heard the chopper circling. Encouraged, he forced himself to move faster.

Then, from somewhere not too far off, he heard Chelsea scream.

* * *

Peyton kept to the trees, but made sure every now and then that he found a break in the canopy so the pursuing chopper pilot could see him.

Inside, he was numb. For fifteen years one thought above all others had kept him going: that he'd eventually be reunited with his boys. He'd even struggled to change his ways so that when he got out, no one — not Bekah, not lawyers, not the courts — could say he wasn't fit to be around decent young men who could perhaps be influenced by their love for him into a life of crime.

And now his dream was over. One son was dead, the other a crazed killer. Where was the justice in that?

Overhead the chopper hovered as the pilot scanned the swamp below for the suspect. Not seeing anyone, the chopper pulled up and swung away as the pilot went in search of another break in the treetops.

It was the chance Peyton was waiting for. Diving under water, he swam back the way he'd come, holding his breath until his lungs threatened to burst; then surfacing, he quickly waded in the direction of Peetre's Pond. With any luck he would catch up with Nash before he harmed the girl. Then he'd do whatever he had to do, no matter what it was, in order to save her.

⋆   ⋆   ⋆

Despite his Pa's instructions, Nash did not head for the tree-house. He knew the FBI would have it staked out by now, and he had too many plans for the future, not just involving this girl but many others, to risk getting captured.

⋆   ⋆   ⋆

Energized by Chelsea's scream, Elliott ran splashing through the swamp toward a stand of moss-draped cypress trees, from behind which the sound had come. He knew he should have been more cautious about attacking an armed madman who obviously killed at will, but he gave no thought to his own safety; his daughter was in grave danger and he was willing to sacrifice his life to save her.

As he got close to the trees, he saw them. They were only a short distance ahead. Chelsea had fallen and Nash was dragging her through knee-deep water by her hair. She was fighting to keep her head above water. It was almost impossible and Elliott could hear her gagging each time she tried to breathe and instead swallowed a mouthful of water.

Enraged, he charged on.

Above the canopy, the helicopter now returned. The loud, uneven thump-thumping of its rotors hid all other noises in the swamp, including the splashing Elliott made as he closed in on Nash and Chelsea.

When Elliott was only a few feet away, Nash heard or sensed someone behind him. He whirled and for an instant looked startled to see Elliott; then, releasing Chelsea, he grabbed for the Glock tucked into his waistband.

A second later Elliott dove for him.

That second cost him. He was too late.

Nash managed to raise the gun and fire just as Elliott landed on him. The bullet hit Elliott high in the chest, buckling him. Both men went sprawling, for a moment lost in the muddy water.

Chelsea, who'd screamed when the gun went off, now waded in to help her father. Blood from his wound was already reddening the water. She could see her father was getting the worst of the fight and she tried desperately to drag Nash away as he and Elliott thrashed around.

It did little good. Badly weakened by his wound, Elliott was no match for Nash. Battered by blows, Elliott grappled with Nash, at the same time yelling for Chelsea to run for it.

She ignored him. And as Nash grabbed her father by the throat and pushed him underwater, she jumped on his back and pounded on him with her fists. Releasing Elliott, Nash reached back and tore her loose. He then hurled her aside and as Elliott came gasping back to the surface, joined his hands together into one big fist and hammered Elliott in the face.

Elliott collapsed, stunned, giving Nash time to reach into the shallow water and pick up his gun.

Chelsea screamed as she saw Nash aiming the gun at her father. Jumping up, she frantically tried to reach him before he could pull the trigger. But she was still a step away when Nash pressed the gun against Elliott's head —

Another gun fired.

A bullet hit Nash in the shoulder, spinning him around. Shocked, he cried out in pain, then turned and saw Kate standing some twenty paces away, her gun still aimed at him.

'FBI!' she yelled. 'Drop the gun!'

'Do it,' Rosy said, approaching from another angle. 'Drop it! Now!'

Nash dropped the Glock and fled.

Kate and Rosy both fired. They only had time for one quick shot. By then Nash was swallowed up by the under-growth.

Kate, already on the move, indicated Chelsea and Elliott, 'Take care of them, homey,' and was gone before Rosy could argue.

For a moment he was tempted to ignore the order and follow the woman he cared most about. Before he could, Chelsea, crouched by her father, begged: 'Please ... he's bleeding ... help me ...'

Relenting, Rosy holstered his gun and went to her side.

41

Kate elbowed her way through the undergrowth, branches whipping her face. She was now running in ankle-deep water. Just ahead was a narrow sandbar. Nash's footprints limped across it. She followed them, and a trail of blood spots, into the woods beyond.

Once in the trees she slowed to a walk. She could neither see nor hear Nash, but his footprints were still visible in the spongy, waterlogged earth. Alongside them, the blood spots were larger and more frequent now, and Kate knew Nash must be badly hit. She also knew he must be weakening, perhaps even dying, but she wasn't about to let her guard down.

A huge uprooted cypress blocked her path. It was overgrown with moss and vines and flowering orchids, proof that it had lain there for years if not centuries. Unable to see over the massive trunk, she approached it cautiously, ready to shoot if

Nash jumped up on the other side. As she got close, she noticed a splash of blood reddening the white petals of a tree orchid and thought: *so he's definitely come this way.*

She inched closer, craning her neck to see over the trunk. Nothing moved. But she glimpsed something blue, something man-made lying on the ground — Nash's denim coveralls, she thought — and got ready to squeeze the trigger.

In that same instant Nash burst out of the nearby bushes. Naked and bloody, gut-hook knife held high, he was on her before she could shoot. Both went sprawling. The fall knocked the gun from Kate's hand. There was no time to find it — Nash was already on top of her, trying to stab her. Crossing her forearms into a V, she thrust them upward and blocked the wrist of his knife-hand. In his weakened state he couldn't overpower her and she managed to heave him off.

She was up first. And as Nash weakly staggered to his feet, she grabbed the hand holding the knife and bent it back toward him. Grunting with pain, he dropped the knife. Kate continued to bend his hand backward, trying to force him to the ground. Nash buckled; then with a final surge of strength, kneed her in the stomach.

Kate doubled over, sucking air, and was driven back by his fist. She stumbled and went down.

Nash picked up his knife and weakly started for her. Then, hearing the helicopter approaching overhead, he turned and limped off.

★　★　★

Nash staggered on, following a thin natural trail that curved alongside the water. Though he was in too much pain to realize it, this was the same path where he'd confronted little Marie Gaspard. Mind in a blur, he suddenly became vaguely aware of a man standing ahead of him.

Nash blinked, wondering if he was dreaming. 'P-Pa,' he said. 'Pa, is that you?'

'Yes, son.' Peyton looked at his boy, once his favorite, and again thought:

Fifteen years . . . Then he said: 'The girl — where is she?'

Before Nash could answer, a large 'gator lunged out of the reeds. It struck before he could react; then, even as he screamed and fell, it dragged him back into the water.

Peyton watched, dumbstruck, as his son vanished from sight. Then instinct kicked in and he started forward, determined to save him.

But even as he ran, he wondered if he was saving Nash from one fate only to deliver him to another — a life behind bars.

Save his life or watch him die?

The decision was almost impossible to make.

42

Kate arrived a few minutes later and stopped at the spot where the 'gator had grabbed Nash. Dragmarks showed in the damp earth, and as she followed them with her eyes she saw a rare sight: a 'gator feeding frenzy.

More than a dozen alligators were fighting each other for scraps of flesh, their gyrating bodies and thrashing tails churning the blood-stained water.

For a few moments Kate watched them with morbid fascination. Then she noticed something floating among the reeds at the water's edge. She found a stick and fished the little bundle out of the water. She guessed what it contained and momentarily hesitated to open it; then, gathering her emotions, she set it down on the trail and untied the once-white handkerchief . . . revealing Ma's ears and tongue.

She looked back at the drag-marks and read the story they told: Nash had somehow been grabbed by a 'gator and was now the object of the feeding frenzy. It seemed a fitting end for a man who'd worshipped a crocodile god, but she derived no pleasure or satisfaction from it. She would have preferred to arrest the Bayou Butcher, not preside over the feast he'd become.

43

'The important thing is that you got him,' said Elliott.

He looked up at Kate and Rosy from a bed at Slidell Memorial Hospital. The bullet had been successfully removed from his chest and he was expected, in time, to make a full recovery.

Though he was still groggy from the anesthetic, he'd insisted on hearing the full story when Kate and Rosy came by to check on him.

'We didn't get him,' Kate said. 'The 'gators did.'

'Still, he's dead, Doc,' said Rosy, 'and that's all that counts.'

Elliott nodded. 'What about the old man . . . Peyton?'

'Vanished,' Rosy said.

'But there's a warrant out for his arrest,' Kate added, 'and the local police have put an APB out on him. We'll catch him sooner or later, but it's not going to be easy. He's at home in that swamp. He could lose himself in there forever.'

'So it's over,' Elliott said.

Kate nodded.

The door opened and Chelsea entered, accompanied by Dr Schulman, the physician who'd just finished examining her.

Elliott tried to sit up, but it was too painful. Wincing, he flopped back on the pillow. Chelsea leaned over and was about to hug him when she remembered his surgery.

'Hey,' Elliott said, opening his arms to her. 'No pain, no gain.'

Chelsea smiled and gently embraced him. 'Love you, Dad.'

'Love you too, Chels'.' He looked over her shoulder at Dr Schulman and asked: 'How is she?'

'Fine.'

'See,' Chelsea said, stepping back. 'I told you I was all right.'

'Thanks for humoring me, anyway,' he said.

As Chelsea started to reply, her cell phone buzzed. She checked the caller ID and quickly answered. 'Bra-ad! Hi! Did you get my message?' To Elliott she mouthed, *It's Brad,* and hurriedly left the room.

Elliott rolled his eyes. 'Guess we all know where I rate.'

Dr Schulman laughed. 'Don't sell yourself short, Dr Ward. The whole time I was examining your daughter, she never stopped talking about you.'

'Me?' he said, surprised. 'Are you sure you examined the right Chelsea?'

'I'm not going to repeat what she said,' Dr Schulman continued, 'because it would only embarrass you. But let's just say that if they made a movie of your life right now, they'd have to call it *Dad of the Year.*'

'That's what you get for saving her life,' Kate said. 'In her eyes that makes you the coolest dad around.'

Elliott felt as if a great weight had been lifted from him. Maybe he hadn't failed her as much as he'd thought.

After Dr Schulman left, he looked at Kate and said: 'That leaves just one thing to iron out — us.'

Before Kate could say anything, Rosy said: 'Guess that's my cue to leave you two alone.' Shaking Elliott's hand, he added: 'Remember, Doc, caution's the way.'

'So I've learned,' Elliott said, 'thanks to you.' He waited until Rosy had left, then turned to Kate. 'He's one hell of a guy.'

'I know,' she said. 'I tell myself that every day.'

Elliott was quiet a moment. Then he pressed his hand over hers, saying: 'About that extended leave of absence you mentioned — '

'What about it?'

'Are you still planning to take it?'

She hesitated. 'I've been thinking about that . . . '

'And?'

'Maybe now's not the best time.'

'I thought you wanted us to take time out — the three of us.'

'I do. I mean, I *did* . . . ' Again she hesitated. 'It's just . . . I was forced to take time off before this case started. In fact, if it hadn't been for Rosy, I'd still be painting the beams in my bedroom ceiling.'

'That doesn't sound so bad,' Elliott said. 'The way my schedule's been lately, I'd love to have some free time.'

'You don't understand,' Kate said. 'I was almost a basket case when Rosy showed up and — '

' — rescued you?'

'Something like that.'

'I'm sure he was glad to do it,' Elliott said with a hint of jealousy. 'I'd fight to keep you on my team, too.'

Kate didn't answer. She wanted to explain that Rosy had done it for her, not himself. He'd known her well enough to know that being isolated on that remote cliff top was not the way to exorcise her demons; only being back on the job could do that. But she realized it wouldn't make any difference. Elliott would probably never understand her like Rosy did. Rosy knew what made her tick; what made her the way she was. She didn't think Elliott would ever understand her that well. What's more, she wasn't sure she wanted him to.

'Elliott,' she began and stopped.

'Go ahead,' he said. 'I want to kn

how you really feel.'

It took her a moment to find the words. 'There was a time when I thought it would work between us.'

'So did I,' he said. 'And now?'

'I don't think so.'

'You don't think so because you *really* don't think so, or because you don't *want* to think so?'

'I don't think so because I realized that both of us are too deeply entrenched in our everyday lives to just give everything up — everything we've worked so hard to achieve — and start again.'

'Why would we have to give everything up? You could always be an agent in New York.'

'You could always practice in Virginia.'

Elliott smiled without humor. 'I see what you mean.'

'I'm just trying to be realistic,' Kate said, wondering as she spoke if she was making the mistake of her life. 'You do understand that, don't you?'

'All too well,' Elliott said grimly. 'Problem is, there's nothing realistic about love. It's a totally *un*realistic yet

340

magical emotion that you either have for someone or you don't. Unfortunately for me, I have it for you, Kate. And I think I always will.'

Kate sighed, torn up inside.

'Are you sure you don't feel the same about me?'

'No,' she said, 'I'm not sure. I'm not sure about anything.'

'Except that you're not willing to give us a chance?'

'Not right now, Elliott, no.'

'Well,' he said, dejected, 'maybe next time.'

Before Kate could reply, her cell vibrated. Startled, she dug it out of her pocket, saw the caller was Rosy, and answered. 'Yeah?'

'I hate to break things up, *jefe*, but we do have a plane to catch.'

'Be right there.' Kate ended the call, and found Elliott watching her intently. 'Gotta run.'

He nodded. 'Will I ever see you again?'

'I hope so.' She bent and kissed him on the forehead, not trusting herself to kiss his lips. 'Take care of yourself, Elliott. And give Chelsea a big hug.'

'Will do,' Elliott said. 'She'll miss you.' He waited until she opened the door, then added: 'Kate . . . it was great seeing you again.'

'You, too.' She smiled and left.

★ ★ ★

Rosy was waiting in the car for her outside the hospital. Kate climbed inside without a word and buckled her seat-belt. Her expression told him how much turmoil she was in.

'You okay, boss?'

'I will be,' she replied.

Starting the car, he pulled out of the hospital driveway and drove in the direction of the airport.

They did not speak again until they were pulling into the rental-car parking lot. Then she said: 'Back at the hospital — do you want to know what Elliott and I decided?'

'Only if you're going to request a transfer to New York.'

'That's not in my future.'

Inside, Rosy relaxed. Parking in one of

the empty stalls, he turned off the engine. Both of them got out and walked to the rear of the car to collect their bags.

As he popped the trunk, he caught her looking at him as if trying to figure something out.

'What?' he asked.

'I was just thinking,' Kate said.

'Uh-oh.'

' — wondering what it was that I really appreciated about you.'

'That's easy. I'm cute and funny and *muy inteligente*.'

He expected her to laugh. When she didn't, he knew how much she must be hurting inside.

'I appreciate you,' she said soberly, 'because you never judge me or press me for answers . . . and you always let me be myself.' Before he could respond she impulsively gave him a quick kiss on the cheek. Then grabbing her bag from the trunk, she set it down on its wheels and started for the terminal.

'Hey,' Rosy called after her. 'Never mind the compliments, *Jefe*, what about my tip?'

44

It didn't take Nash long to break into Leblanc's supply room. The hasp on the door was old and rusty, and wedging the blade of his hook-end knife behind it, he easily broke it open.

Entering, he flipped on the light, squinting until his eyes adjusted to the glare. He was still naked under his father's old Confederate coat and the first thing he helped himself to was a pair of jeans, a shirt, socks and hiking boots. He then filled a bag full of bandages and medicines to help heal his wounds.

After he was dressed, he raided the shelves of canned foods, a flashlight, and a whetstone to keep his knife sharp, then threw everything into a sack and limped out into the cool, dark night.

He knew he was a lucky man. Just when it seemed to him that there was no way out, Pa had come to his rescue, sacrificed his own life so that Nash might live. Now, with Pa gone, he had only one debt to pay, and that was to Sobek. He still owed the ancient god the remaining sacrifices for returning Pa to him — if only for a brief time. Eighteen people still had to die. And they had to die in threes.

All he needed now was to compile his list of victims. He wasn't sure yet who those victims would be — except for the first three.

The girl, Chelsea, her father, Dr Ward, and of course that FBI agent. He couldn't remember her name, but her face was burned into his memory.

Oh, how he'd enjoy himself once he had *her* under his knife . . .

We do hope that you have enjoyed reading this large print book.

Did you know that all of our titles are available for purchase?

We publish a wide range of high quality large print books including:
**Romances, Mysteries, Classics
General Fiction
Non Fiction and Westerns**

Special interest titles available in large print are:
**The Little Oxford Dictionary
Music Book, Song Book
Hymn Book, Service Book**

Also available from us courtesy of Oxford University Press:
**Young Readers' Dictionary
(large print edition)
Young Readers' Thesaurus
(large print edition)**

For further information or a free brochure, please contact us at:
**Ulverscroft Large Print Books Ltd.,
The Green, Bradgate Road, Anstey,
Leicester, LE7 7FU, England.
Tel:** (00 44) **0116 236 4325
Fax:** (00 44) **0116 234 0205**

MARKED FOR MURDER

Norman Lazenby

'Leave this affair alone, Martinson — Jean Hallison is dead . . . ' The caller had rung off, leaving Inspector Jim Martinson wondering if this was a bluff. Had Jean been murdered? And where did the suave, grinning Montoni fit in? He was accused of assaulting two women — but at the same time Jim himself had been watching him elsewhere. Now, however, Jim links the chain of evidence — slowly tightening the rope that will bring in the sinister gang that is terrorising Framcastle.

BURY THE HATCHET

John Russell Fearn

George Carter and his family lived peacefully in the small town of Uphill. But one fateful weekend something caused them to experience real fear and act completely out of character. The first trigger was when they learned that a homicidal maniac was at large in Uphill, carrying a damaged suitcase containing his victim's body parts. The second trigger was on finding that their new lodger's suitcase was also damaged — and the grisly truth of what was inside . . .

EXPERIMENT IN MURDER

John Russell Fearn

Moore dreams he's in the Lake District, climbing a mountain — carrying a woman's body — the woman he attacked as she slept in their hotel. He throws her body into the chasm at the summit and returns to the hotel. He wakes up. He examines his shoes: just as he left them before retiring, no trace of mud from the hillside . . . then it *has* all been a dream! But Moore, victim of an experiment in murder, finds his dream is real!

KILLER SMILE

Steve Hayes & David Whitehead

Jack Monroe's dream was to start a foundation that would encourage architects from poorer families. But to achieve this dream he would need fifty million dollars. So he hooked up with the wealthy Thornhill family. But the Thornhills had more than their share of dirty secrets, and Jack found himself a pawn in a deadly game of murder and deceit. Now, he would need to take the utmost care not to become the architect of his own downfall.

MR. BUDD STEPS IN

Gerald Verner

Somewhere in England is a steel box — its contents more valuable than diamonds — that Superintendent Robert Budd must find. Budd's investigation takes him to Higher Wicklow, where a tramp had sheltered in its reputedly haunted mill. Some days later, his body was discovered, his throat cut. Although the coroner's verdict was suicide, the villagers believe there's a more sinister explanation. Can the Superintendent discover the truth? Budd's heavy caseload also includes murder, ghostly goings on, a vanishing and blackmail.

THE DARK GATEWAY

John Burke

In a lonely corner of Wales, an ancient castle quivers with evil as menacing powers return from beyond . . . The family living on the hillside farm with their daughter, Nora, has a stranger coming to live with them. But he's not what he seems — he will not fulfil Nora's hopes of romance . . . As the powers of darkness approach, the human race is in danger and the earth itself is at stake. In this frightened community, who will oppose the invaders?